"I do not recall you being so dramatic, Matilda. Isolation has not agreed with you."

"On the contrary, isolation has introduced me to myself. Isolation has given me *everything*. I have no reason to believe marriage will offer me much of anything. I refuse, Javier. I will not go to Spain with you. I will not find someone to marry. I have a hard time imagining you showing up with a priest on my twenty-fifth birthday demanding I marry *you*. So, we are at an impasse."

She had the oddest image of him here now that she'd spoken it. Marrying Javier. Him living in her tiny cottage among all her plants. The dangerous energy pumping off him, even when he pretended to be relaxed and acting in her best interest, would incinerate them both.

"If you do not do this, Matilda," he said, his voice low and harsh, "I will cut you off. Financially, as is the stipulation of the will. Furthermore, I will cut you out of WB Industries altogether. You will have nothing."

For ticking seconds, Matilda could only stare at him, a strange kind of numbness settling over her.

"The stipulation of the will is that if I do not marry by twenty-five, you have to marry me. You cannot cut me off, Javier. You will have to marry me."

Lorraine Hall is a part-time hermit and full-time writer. She was born with an old soul and her head in the clouds, which, it turns out, is the perfect combination to spend her days creating thunderous alpha heroes and the fierce, determined heroines who win their hearts. She lives in a potentially haunted house with her soulmate and rambunctious band of hermits-in-training. When she's not writing romance, she's reading it.

Books by Lorraine Hall

Harlequin Presents

The Prince's Royal Wedding Demand
A Son Hidden from the Sicilian
The Forbidden Princess He Craves
Playing the Sicilian's Game of Revenge

Secrets of the Kalyva Crown

Hired for His Royal Revenge
Pregnant at the Palace Altar

Visit the Author Profile page
at Harlequin.com.

A Diamond for His Defiant Cinderella

LORRAINE HALL

HARLEQUIN®
PRESENTS™

Recycling programs for this product may not exist in your area.

ISBN-13: 978-1-335-59340-5

A Diamond for His Defiant Cinderella

Copyright © 2024 by Lorraine Hall

For questions and comments about the quality of this book, please contact us at CustomerService@Harlequin.com.

TM and ® are trademarks of Harlequin Enterprises ULC.

Harlequin Enterprises ULC
22 Adelaide St. West, 41st Floor
Toronto, Ontario M5H 4E3, Canada
www.Harlequin.com

Printed in Lithuania

MIX
Paper | Supporting responsible forestry
FSC® C021394

A Diamond for His Defiant Cinderella

CHAPTER ONE

JAVIER ALATORRE GOT out of his sleek rental car and immediately stepped into a thick, cold puddle of mud. He scowled up at the drizzling gray sky, then at his now-ruined shoe.

He could not fathom why anyone would live in this isolated, wild place when they could have everything at their fingertips in sunny Spain.

But Matilda had wanted this, and after a rather disastrous series of events, he'd allowed it. As a kindness, as a gift. He had not bothered her while she'd spent three years holed away in this place, and he wasn't particularly keen on doing so now.

But the time for licking her wounds was over. Time was ticking.

He'd known Matilda Willoughby for nearly a decade now. He'd never been able to think of her as a *sister*, though Ewan Willoughby had been an excellent father figure to him in the years he'd been involved with and then married to Javier's mother.

Javier had been sixteen when his mother had begun seeing Ewan. Though his mother wouldn't agree to marry Ewan for another five years, Ewan had acted as a father to Javier almost immediately.

In those early years, Ewan had changed Javier from an angry, potentially violent scrapper into a polished, sophisticated businessman. He'd encouraged Javier to attend university, he had secured Javier an entry-level job at WB Industries before he'd graduated, and then he'd set him on the path to heir apparent. Ewan had polished all of Javier's rough edges, taught him the delicate art of control and turned him into the man he was today.

It hadn't been until his parents' engagement that he'd met Matilda. A shy teen who'd preferred hiding behind her father and spending her years at boarding school rather than concern herself with Javier.

Then the unexpected and unthinkable had happened. Ewan had died suddenly, with no warning, no chance for Javier to prepare. Javier hadn't just lost his father figure. He hadn't just gotten a promotion and a business he had to ensure succeeded for the man who'd left it to him.

He'd become the guardian of a sixteen-year-old. One he'd barely known. He could have counted on one hand the number of times he'd been in the same room as Matilda at that time.

But he'd taken such a strange responsibility seriously all the same, endeavoring to keep Matilda's life as smooth as it had been when her father was alive. He ensured she finished school, kept her incredibly complicated and hefty finances in order, and set her up in a nice house with his mother when she wasn't at university. All while he took the reins of Ewan's company and made it even *more* impressive.

He would not fail Ewan's memory, the man who'd changed the course of his life. He would not allow all the warped ugliness of his childhood to change that. Which was why control was always the name of the game.

He sighed, studying the little cottage Matilda had been calling home instead of his mother's house in Valencia. Part of his control was keeping adult Matilda out of his orbit, for reasons he didn't care to dwell on.

Now he needed to call upon all his control to do what needed doing.

Javier straightened his jacket and moved for the door. If the day were more pleasant, perhaps he could have called it picturesque. But today the cottage simply looked gray and incapable of keeping the cold out with its rustic stones and dilapidated-looking roof.

Much like living in this cottage, Matilda had never made much sense to him. Her obsession with plants. Her sweet, trusting nature. Her preference to be alone. *This.*

Three years ago she'd suffered a great embarrassment, yes, and her inheritance meant that she was *quite* notorious simply for the amount of money she had. But Javier could never understand *hiding away,* just because the man she'd been engaged to had turned out to be a scheming, lying gold digger.

The press had been a bit relentless, and they'd painted her an empty-headed fool, but the daughter of Ewan Willoughby should have had thicker skin, in Javier's estimation.

But he'd done what he thought Ewan might in the situation. He'd allowed Matilda to buy this little cottage in the Scottish Highlands. He'd given her time and space to do what she pleased for the time allotted.

It had been easier with her far away than it had been when she'd been gallivanting about Spain on the arm of

Pietro the traitor. Showing up at events he was at, looking every inch a *woman*, and not a child to be guarded.

But those years were long gone, and Javier did not have to understand her to make certain she was taken care of, and now, that she lived out the requirements of her father's will and last wishes. Because he *was* her guardian, no matter how old or anything else she was.

Before he could make it to the door, he heard the sounds of someone approaching from behind. He turned to find Matilda striding up a muddy trail.

She wore layers of wool and knitwear, much of it as muddy as the trail. Her curly auburn hair had likely been pulled back at some point, but most of it had fallen out of the band and whipped about her flushed face.

He had not seen her in person for over a year. Perhaps it was closer to two now. He'd chosen to vacation in Capri rather than return to his mother's home for Christmas where the two women had gathered.

Ever since her twenty-first birthday party, shining and happy on Pietro's arm, Javier had refused to name the thing that wormed through him at the sight of her. Her red hair, her violet eyes, her slim form. She was an attractive woman, and any reaction within him was simply a product of biology.

Nothing more.

She carried a strange basket filled to the brim with plants and she swung it as she walked, humming a little tune despite the wet, dreary day. She did not seem to notice him standing there until she was practically upon him. Then she stopped abruptly.

"Javier." She blinked. She did not smile, as she might

have once at his arrival. He immediately saw a wariness in her nearly violet eyes, like she knew exactly why he was here.

Which would hurry things along.

"Matilda. You have been avoiding my calls."

"And emails," she added, somewhat cheerfully. She brushed past him and headed for the cottage door. She unlocked it, wiping her muddy boots on an equally muddy mat outside the door.

So much mud, Javier half feared what would be found inside.

"You needn't have come all this way," she said, stepping inside. She hung the basket on a hook, then went about removing some of her layers.

The cottage was warm, not frigid as he'd imagined. He'd give her that as he stepped inside. It was also…to call it "cluttered" would be a kindness. It looked like a science experiment gone awry, which was Matilda's calling card, in fairness.

"I would have much preferred to stay where I was, warm and dry and all, but again. You were not returning my correspondence."

She sighed heavily, then held out a hand. "Would you like me to take your coat?"

He looked at the hooks along the wall. All hanging with wet and muddy clothes, or baskets filled with dirt and green. "No. Thank you."

She laughed, and at least there was that. She had found her good humor once again out here, instead of being the pale, devastated girl of three years ago.

He had not liked that at all.

"Tea?" she asked, moving into the tiny kitchen. He had no idea how she'd even find a kettle.

"No, Matilda. I have my plane waiting. You may take as long as you'd like to pack." He glanced at the acres of plants. Living, dried, halfway between life and death. "Perhaps we can hire someone from the village to take care of your…garden while you are gone."

"I do not plan on going anywhere, Javier," she said quite firmly as she produced a kettle from who-knew-where.

He didn't care for the firmness in her tone. This was another new piece of her. She had once been quite obedient. Now she'd had too much time alone. Too much independence. Better than being a doormat, he supposed, but the behavior did not suit his current purposes.

"Whether you plan on it or not, you will be returning to Spain with me. You will be twenty-five in six months, so there is much to do to find you an appropriate husband."

She slammed the kettle and glared at him. "You can't be serious with all this."

"I apologize, *cariño*, but *I* do not plan on marrying you. So we must work on finding someone suitable. Six months is not much time."

"Honestly, Javier." Every step of making tea was done with jerky, angry movements. Not the Matilda he was familiar with. "I know my father put that ridiculous term in his will or whatever, but I have no plans on seeing it through. Surely no court would enforce it, and who would sue me for being single?" She glared up at him again. "You?"

"It is what your father wished, so it will be done."

"He isn't here, is he?"

He wanted to be annoyed with her, but he heard enough

grief in her tone, even though she kept it out of her eyes, that he tried to maintain some patience. Ewan had always insisted it was a virtue.

Javier had yet to fully accept that, but he was doing his best.

"He entrusted me with this, Matilda. I am sorry I cannot be more amenable to your opinion on the matter. Your father wanted you married, and so you shall be. But never fear. I will help you."

"Not by marrying me, of course. Too much wantoning about the continent to do?"

He smiled at her, a smile that had most women in his orbit either blushing or disrobing. "Precisely."

"I do not wish to be married," Matilda insisted, doing neither, which was for the best, of course. "Even if I did, there is simply no way to ensure that it's because someone loves *me*, not my bank account."

"Pietro was one man, Matilda," he said, with all the limited gentleness in him.

"Do not speak his name in my house." There wasn't so much anger behind that admonition as there was hurt, and Javier had no interest in diving into *that*. He'd never understood why she couldn't find her anger in the situation. Her fighting spirit.

Toward Pietro, of course. Not him.

"We will go to Spain. I will find you a husband who does not have any designs on your money."

"You cannot simply trot me about Spain and expect me to find love in six months."

Javier did not think she needed to find love so much as she needed to find a good match. A partner. Perhaps one who would not look around this cottage and see the horror he did.

Ewan had not *loved* Javier's mother, so much as the man had saved her. It had been…friendship over passion. It was why it had taken his mother so long to agree to marry Ewan. She had not trusted *love*. Love was what had made his entire childhood hell.

Still, Javier knew better than to argue intangibles when he had tangibles to accomplish. "Perhaps not, but you will definitely not find it playing the role of hermit out here."

"I am doing botany."

"I have gardens in Spain. You may do botany there. While you find yourself a husband."

She rolled her eyes, then closed them. She sucked in a deep breath, then let it out slowly. When she opened her eyes, the unique violet landed in him strangely. An edge of something that he wrote off as frustration that she was making this more difficult than she should be.

Always frustration with her because he would not allow it to be anything else. *Control.* No one did it better than Javier Alatorre.

"Javier. I appreciate that you've taken time out of your busy schedule running my father's company and sleeping your way through Europe, but I am quite content to stay right here. I have no intention of marrying *anyone*, and while I appreciate your dedication to my father's memory, as much as I love and miss him, he was not a perfect man and his decision to put this into his will was wrong. If I ever marry, it will be on my own time, of my own will."

Javier had learned years ago, at the hand of this woman's father, how to control the temper his monster of a biological father had left to him. To contain the roiling anger inside him, the monster inside him, somewhere else.

But she poked at all the lessons he'd learned. He wanted to shout at her. Throw a few of her colorful pots against the wall and watch them crash into a thousand tiny pieces. The kind of battles that even all these years removed from them felt more comfortable than the peace Ewan Willoughby had offered him and his mother.

But he did not give into those old impulses, bred in him by a violent father. He would never unleash such a horror on Matilda. *That* is why he preferred her countries away.

But for the next six months, he would have to muster all his control, all his patience. Because he would not fail Ewan. So he breathed, and he smiled.

"Unfortunately, Matilda, you are incorrect. You have no free will."

Mattie had lived on this planet for almost eight years without her father, and still she missed him with a deep, throbbing ache. But missing him did not mean she couldn't curse his name for this thing he'd done to her.

Javier Alatorre being the looming guardian who wouldn't go away had never been *comfortable*, but Mattie had never *hated* it until now. Mostly, Javier had been hands-off. In the years she'd gone to university in Barcelona, their paths had crossed more frequently, but Pietro had always been with her. It had felt like a…strange little safety blanket.

Not that she felt unsafe with Javier exactly. Just on edge. Never quite sure where she stood. He could be so…opaque.

It did not matter. Not then. Not now. She had built a

life for herself in the ashes of her last one. She was not the same woman who'd had her heart crushed, her humiliated face plastered across every tabloid and website interested in the doings of the incredibly wealthy.

She had thrown herself into studying plants, into creating a life that made her happy. Into a life that kept her firmly out of any public's interest.

Maybe cutting off any friends she'd had *before*, and basically only communicating with her stepmother, Elena, on any kind of regular basis for the past three years had left her a bit…lonely these days, but some ridiculous marriage Javier facilitated was hardly going to solve *that* problem.

She studied him across the little counter filled to the brim with her plants. Some experiments. Some for fun. She was fascinated by how things grew, what they needed to flourish. And what ended up killing them.

And in the middle of all this green and growth and *her* space was the man who her father had allowed to have far too much power over her.

It should have been Elena. Mattie had never pegged her father for a chauvinist, but making Javier her guardian and putting him in charge of all her finances and her entire future reeked of misogyny.

Now Javier was here, throwing his manly weight around like he got to decide. Invading her space with his broad shoulders and fierce dark eyes.

He had always been handsome, even when his shoulders had not been so broad and he had carried a chip the size of Spain itself on them. But there was something under all those good looks, all that easy charm he'd learned how to employ so successfully.

A current of danger. A thread of something…threatening. She did not know what or why, but she had always known it was in her best interest to steer very clear or to have some kind of buffer—Pietro, Elena.

She'd done an excellent job up to this moment.

Now he wanted her to come with him to Spain. To shop her around like she was a prized cow to be auctioned off.

"How do you suppose you will force me to go to Spain, Javier?" she asked, trying to sound like one of her old professors posing a philosophical question to an audience full of people who hadn't lived long enough to have a philosophical quandary.

"I beg your pardon?"

"I do not want to go. You say I have no free will. So how will you take my will away from me? How will you *force* me to do all these things, when I am refusing to do them? How do you suppose you will—legally and ethically—determine who I will marry? Do you have hidden puppetry skills that will make it seem as though I said *I do* to the man of your choosing? Perhaps you've studied hypnotism and think you can get me down the aisle to a stranger that way?"

His gaze was cool, his expression bland, except for the sharp blade of his mouth. He had fixed a mask of bored indifference onto his face, but he was *here*. He was not taking no for an answer. So, it wasn't all indifference.

"I do not recall you being so dramatic, Matilda. Isolation has not agreed with you."

"On the contrary, isolation has introduced me to myself. Isolation has given me *everything*. I have no reason to believe marriage will offer me much of anything. I refuse, Javier. I will not go to Spain with you. I will not find someone to marry. I have a hard time imagining you showing up with a priest on my twenty-fifth birthday demanding I marry *you*. So we are at an impasse."

She had the oddest image of him here now that she'd spoken it. Marrying Javier. Him living in her tiny cottage among all her plants. The dangerous energy pumping off of him, even when he pretended to be relaxed and acting in her best interest, would incinerate them both.

Not that it would ever come to that. Javier might prize her father's memory, bend over backward to jump through every ridiculous hoop he'd set up at his death, but Javier would never marry the likes of her.

So this was all a very large waste of everyone's time. Surely Javier would see that and leave.

"Would you like to stay for dinner?" she asked. Hoping the homey, cozy offer—both things Javier avoided at all costs according to his mother—would send him packing.

But Javier did not relent. He did not soften. He did not turn tail and run. He stood there, all icy expressions and that throb of something hot and angry that was surely a figment of her overactive imagination.

"If you do not do this, Matilda," he said, his voice low and harsh, "I will cut you off. Financially, as is the stipulation of the will. Furthermore, I will cut you out of WB Industries altogether. You will have nothing."

For ticking seconds, Matilda could only stare at him. A strange kind of numbness settling over her. Shock, perhaps. Outrage would come, but she was too surprised to find it in the moment. Because he was forgetting one very important part of her father's will.

"The stipulation of the will is that if I do not marry by

twenty-five, *you* have to marry me. You cannot cut me off, Javier. You will have to marry me."

But he shook his head. Because he thought he was in charge. Because he thought *she* didn't get to decide her life, but *he* did.

"You have an hour to pack up your things, Matilda."

CHAPTER TWO

JAVIER CONSIDERED THREATS a last resort, but he was running out of patience. If the woman could not honor her father's memory, then he would be harsh. She might find it unfair, but he considered it the *most* fair.

Would Ewan approve of such methods? Javier did not know. But it was never his goal to be a carbon copy of Ewan. Ewan had impressed upon him the importance of being his *own* man, using his *own* strengths to build an empire.

And protect his daughter.

Who seethed in her little kitchen. Muddy and unkempt and surprisingly unruly when she'd always been quite dutiful before.

"I shall set a timer, if you need one."

Those violet eyes narrowed. He did not recognize this version of Matilda, but it was immaterial to his goal. He'd learned not to let himself get distracted or wound up over the immaterial. Over this woman.

"You can go to hell," she said, but she stormed past him and into a room. Slamming the door behind her.

"This isn't very mature of you, Matilda," he called through the door.

He heard the crash of something. Hopefully her beginning to pack. He did not care if she *liked* what she was doing, as long as she did it.

He could admit in the privacy of his own mind that he was a bit surprised by her reaction. It wasn't as though he thought she'd jump for joy, but he assumed she would understand it was a necessity.

Instead, she thought it was…a joke, he supposed. Something to ignore because a "court" would not enforce it. Well, she was right about that, because he would not be forced to marry her or *anyone*. But he would not disappoint Ewan.

He considered his proposition very fair, considering he was giving her the *choice* of suitors, even if not the time she wanted. She was being the unreasonable one, and she was going to have to start falling into line without these surprising little rebellions.

Speaking of rebellion, he realized it had been quiet inside her room for some time.

Suspiciously so. Javier considered the layout of the cottage, then sighed. Preparing himself for the sting of cold, he stepped back outside.

He was not surprised to find her there, climbing out of the window at the back of the cottage. She'd changed clothes. She still wore dull brown and baggy clothes best suited for hiking, but they were no longer muddy. Nor were the boots she wore. Her wild hair had been bundled up under a cap. She looked like some kind of old-fashioned street urchin.

More so when she turned, stopped abruptly, and scowled at him. In one hand she held a little bag. In the other, a pocketknife.

He raised an eyebrow at it. "What are you going to do? Stab me?"

She lifted her chin, but she'd clearly never had to physically defend herself because she was holding it all wrong to be threatening. He would know.

"Maybe."

"You don't even like to kill spiders, Matilda."

"Spiders aren't attempting to ruin my life."

"Clearly isolation has gone to your head. You are inventing dramatics and not behaving like yourself at all."

"Maybe this *is* exactly myself, Javier."

"A pity then. You were much more marriageable before."

"Well, my goal is no longer to be *marriageable*. It is to be *happy*."

Something about the word *happy* settled in him like fury. But he was not a man who used his fury like a weapon. Not anymore. Because of Ewan Willoughby. "And wouldn't you be happier seeing to your father's last wishes? I would be. Stop acting like a spoiled child. Now, if you don't wish to bring anything else of your own to Spain, that's well enough. You certainly have the funds to buy whatever you need. Let us be off then."

"This is insanity, Javier. I don't know what's gotten into you, but if you'd have some sense and simply let this go—"

He stepped forward. She lifted the knife like her chin, but she didn't know how to hold it to do any damage. She'd lived a pampered, sheltered life of a princess, really. She knew nothing about protecting herself from an attack.

Which made him even angrier. He wanted to reach out and shake some sense into her, but he kept his arms at his sides even as he leaned in closer.

"Your father saved the course of my life, Matilda," he said, every word as vicious as a threat. "I owe him everything I am. So, no, I will not simply let this go. Turn away. I will not give up on this. I will find a way to get you married. Now you can come have a say in it, or I can go find a man for you on my own with none of your input. I will not rest until this is accomplished. Do you understand?"

Her eyes had gotten very wide, but she had not stepped back. She had not wilted or scurried off…like he expected her to. She stood her ground, even if her eyes were suspiciously shiny.

"I know you loved him very much," she said, her voice a rough scrape against the frigid cold air around them. "So did I, but he was wrong to do this to me." Her lower lip wobbled, but she firmed it.

He did not think isolation had been good for her, clearly, since she wasn't being sensible. But he would give it one thing. The time alone, or maybe the embarrassment itself, had developed a backbone in Matilda.

It would be good for her, something Ewan would be proud of, but that didn't mean Javier didn't curse the bad timing for *him*.

"If it is wrong in his name, so be it." He took a deep, cleansing breath. He straightened his jacket. Then he pasted a relaxed smile on his face. "Now, will you be getting in the car on your own, or do I need to carry you?"

Mattie was tempted to continue the standoff. But she had no doubt Javier would indeed pick her up. And that would require his hands on her body and she…

Well, *she* might have changed a bit over the past three

years, but the idea of him touching her still felt...dangerous, for ways she didn't allow herself to fully fathom. It was like looking into a black hole. Peer too deeply and she'd get sucked in and disappear forever.

Much like being married off. But she clearly wasn't going to get through to him with reason. So what could she do?

Maybe she should consider it a...vacation. She'd visit Elena, enjoy some time in Spain and then...figure out how to convince Javier she could certainly live the rest of her days without ever getting married and everything would be fine.

She could be rational and logical, even if *he* could not. At least not when it came to her father.

Though the pocketknife in her hand that she used for cuttings and grafting might prove her logic had failed her momentarily. She folded the blade back and slid it into her pocket.

"Ah, so you're ready to be reasonable," he said, with that easy smile she realized was not quite so easy as he pretended. She'd watched him just now. All that vibrating anger and frustration carefully masked.

No, this man was not the easy playboy she'd always assumed. But he *was* the dangerous man she'd always feared. So she'd be careful.

But she wouldn't be the old Matilda. She would not scurry away from him, or behind other people when it came to the strange reactions he stirred in her. She would face him down. She would be her own protector now.

"Reasonable would be leaving me be, but if you feel duty bound to honor my father in this ridiculous way, I'll go along with it for the time being." She began to trudge after him toward his car. "After all, it's been a long time since I saw your mother."

"You will not be staying with my mother. You will be staying with me in Barcelona."

This put a bit of a hitch in her stride. "But… I always stay with Elena when I'm in Spain."

"Yes, when you are vacationing or summering. But this is not a vacation, Matilda. We have a very short period of time to find you a husband and get you married, and I will be overseeing the entire endeavor. So you will stay with me."

With him.

"I hardly think…"

"Let me stop you right there, *cariño*. You do not have to think. You only have to obey."

She considered pulling the knife back out. Maybe it wouldn't do any damage, maybe she'd never actually bring herself to be violent, but it felt more like power than sparring with Javier.

"Be a good girl and get married off like some medieval princess who has no agency, no power and no say?"

"If that is how you wish to look at it. I happen to see it as a privileged woman having to adjust her expectations for the future, for her own good, rather than any kind of *infringement*."

"That is because you are a man, and even a lack of privilege doesn't stop you from making the world yours."

Something flickered in his eyes, and she wasn't so naive anymore to fancy it hurt, or even guilt. No, Javier did not have any emotional attachment to *her*—not as stepbrother, not as guardian. She was simply an inanimate extension of her father to him.

"Get in the car, Matilda. I would like to be home by dinner as some of us have jobs and business to attend to. You've enjoyed all this free time to do whatever you please while you bemoan your lack of agency and power, have you not?"

It wasn't fair of him, nor was it fully off base. She *had* enjoyed a life doing whatever she wished because of her father's money these past few years. But only because she had not been able to face any role in her father's—now Javier's—company after what had happened with Pietro.

She didn't think that meant she should have to go along with what her guardian said when she was twenty-four. An adult. Her own woman who could make her own decisions.

No matter what her father had thought she'd be at this age. Apparently weak and silly and whatever it was that he thought meant she needed a husband as some kind of legal minder.

The thought depressed her, as it always did. Because he was not here for her to yell at him. To demand to know what he'd been thinking. To find answers to why the man who'd always treated her like she was smart, savvy and special had determined that had some kind of shelf life.

And because she was distracted by that feeling, she allowed Javier to usher her into the passenger seat of his rental car. She watched her cottage disappear as Javier drove away.

She knew it was a little childish to pout and sulk, but she thought she'd earned the right to indulge in *some* childishness. As her beloved adopted home passed by outside the car. As all her plants and experiments were left behind.

She had found herself out here. Yes, away from everyone. Yes, *isolated*. It had changed her. Just as Pietro's betrayal had changed her and her father's unexpected death had changed her.

She would not marry just anyone. She wouldn't marry at all. It was ludicrous.

She sneaked a look at Javier. His gaze was intent on the muddy, bumpy roads as he drove. His grip tight on the steering wheel as it tried to jerk this way and that. He was all sleek, controlled power, threat, *danger*.

And she was going along with him. Maybe she could convince him to leave this ridiculous need to see through her father's archaic wishes by virtue of just what she had said to him. She would not go into this worrying about being marriageable, about how the men Javier threw her at perceived her. She would not concern herself with the society manners and hostess smiles she'd been raised to embody.

She would be herself. So firmly and wholly, *no one* would want to marry her.

Maybe then Javier would get it through his thick, grief-warped skull that he did not owe it to her father to make his daughter miserable.

And she would be free once more.

CHAPTER THREE

THE FLIGHT HOME was smooth and uneventful. Javier was a bit frustrated he'd had to make the trip, but it had turned out acceptably. Matilda had come because it had been the easiest course of action and that was the kind of woman she was.

Javier had always thought Ewan wanting her married off *was* a bit old-fashioned and unnecessary, if Javier gave it any thought at all. Mostly, he considered it his duty regardless of his own opinions on the matter.

He certainly wasn't going to marry her. Ewan had put that in there, but Javier knew that it must have been some kind of incentive to find someone else for her. Ewan knew him too well to want him for his precious daughter. So, he wanted someone else, and had been smart enough to put something in there to make sure Javier accomplished this for him.

Matilda's recent behavior made him think perhaps Ewan's instincts had been right on about getting her married. She needed someone to usher her through the difficulties of life, lest she be tossed about like a buoy at sea. She could not always run away and hide when bad things happened. She would need to learn to face life's difficulties now, and perhaps a husband was just the way to teach her that.

Perhaps she would not be grateful to him for ensuring her father's wishes were met, but she should be.

They switched from plane to car once they landed in Barcelona, and Javier took the drive himself. While he appreciated his staff, and the luxuries money could buy, he prized his control when it made sense to.

He drove them to the sprawling, ancient estate outside of Barcelona he'd purchased a few years ago from some minor royal. He'd never invited Matilda here. He barely even allowed his mother. It was *his* place. *His* world. For him and his small staff. No family. No women.

If Javier ever saw Matilda in Spain, it was at the house Ewan had bought his mother in Valencia. And he'd avoided those little get-togethers because they'd felt...

He had no words for it. When Ewan was alive, the man had felt like a...coach, perhaps. A leader.

Without him, it felt as though Javier was supposed to step into those shoes. To be the head of the family. And every time that thought took hold, he looked down at his hands and saw his biological father's fists there.

He did not look down at his hands on the steering wheel now. He focused on the road, the turn and then the meandering drive up to his house, where he allowed no ghosts of a past he'd banished long ago.

Matilda would have to stay with him now for as long as this took. It was the only way to ensure this went off without a hitch, so that is what would be done.

Javier parked in the front and carried her meager bag for her. Luis was waiting at the door. The man acted as Javier's right-hand man at the estate and was one of the few people Javier trusted implicitly.

He took the stairs, handed Matilda's bag off to Luis, but Matilda did not follow. Javier frowned as he turned to see her inspecting the plant that grew and flowered over the archway at the beginning of the stairs.

"Have her bag put in her room, Luis. We will eat out on the terrace momentarily."

Luis took the bag and nodded, disappearing into the house to instigate the dinner preparations.

Then, keeping his irritation on the back burner, Javier retraced his steps and met Matilda underneath the arbor and the vine she was inspecting.

"Javier, I had no idea. Your mother made it sound… dreary." Her hand trailed over a climbing plant that twisted around the arbor. "It's beautiful."

An odd tension took residence in his chest. He knew his mother found this much space for one man its own kind of hermitage, but she did not understand. The fact Matilda seemed to…

Was irrelevant, of course. She *was,* in fact, a hermit. Naturally she would find little wrong with the refuge he'd built himself. At least *his* choice of isolation was on a paved street, near a populated city, within driving distance of anything a man of his stature could want. And he held a job, dealt with people day in and day out.

He was no hermit.

"I had no idea you had such a green thumb," Matilda continued.

"It is not mine. I have an excellent gardening staff." The

amount of plants and whatnot that had come with the house had required such.

"I don't recall you ever having any interest in plants."

"I do not. The house came with them, and so they are well tended." He did not ever spend any time asking himself why he'd been so drawn to the house with extensive gardening needs when he had no vested interest in such things. He certainly wouldn't start now.

"I believe you were complaining of being hungry not all that long ago?" he prompted.

"I always forget my hunger in the face of interesting plants."

"Perhaps you have just been away from good food for too long." He took her arm, a gesture that might have once felt paternalistic, but it was harder and harder to pretend as though she was the teenager he'd first met all those years ago when his duty was to find her a husband.

He had to be able to view her as a woman so he could find the appropriate match for her. As much as his goal was to see her married, it would not be to a scam artist like Pietro, or someone who would treat her poorly. That was definitely not what Ewan would have wanted.

Javier had no use for *love*, and wasn't all that sure that *happy* mattered either. He wasn't sure what Ewan would have felt about either— this was not covered in their conversations in Javier's young adulthood. Still, he knew Ewan wanted his daughter taken care of. Content, if not happy.

So Javier would endeavor to find that for her, no matter how difficult she was about the whole matter. He finally coaxed her away from the plants and inside. He led her through the house to the guest wing where she would have free rein over a series of rooms. He took her through all of them, ending with the opulent bedroom with a terrace where his staff had set up a nice evening meal.

She did a slow circle in the middle of the room as if taking everything in. "Javier, this is…too much."

He raised an eyebrow at her. "You forget I know that your childhood home was essentially a castle."

She sighed a little at that. "I suppose it was, but it was my home. And I was a child. I had no sense of what it took or cost to keep such a space taken care of. Now I do."

"Do not concern yourself with cost. You are a guest. As such, you shall be afforded the best. It is not as if I can't afford it."

She frowned at that, but she did meander out onto the terrace to observe the table of food. She eyed the layout with some interest. "Your mother did say you have the best cook in all of Europe."

"Yes, she should know, as she routinely tries to steal Emil away from me."

Matilda smiled at this. "That does sound like Elena." She eyed the setup, then him across the room, still inside. "Aren't you going to eat with me?"

"I have much to do this evening since I had to waste my day flying to Scotland."

She scowled at him. "You didn't *have* to. You could have let me be."

He waved this away.

Matilda walked back into the room and toward him, still wearing her drab hiking clothes. Her hair once again wild. Those violet eyes studying him with an expression he did not wish to discern. She looked so strange here, in the midst of all his chosen opulence, a dull, brown sore thumb, aside from her hair and eyes.

Which made no sense. She'd been born and raised rich as they came. She could belong in any room she chose. He would not concern himself with why she chose to hide herself away.

Or why those violet eyes on him almost made him uncomfortable, when it was *his* house, and *his* space, and all that lay before him were *his* choices.

"Eat and get some rest, Matilda. It is sure to be a long six months." And with that, he turned on a heel and left her there.

Because nothing got to haunt him here. Not even the living.

Mattie couldn't sleep. For a wide variety of reasons. She wasn't the greatest sleeper in the best of times, so she was more philosophical about the situation than frustrated at her whirling mind.

The meal she'd eaten by herself in complete silence had been delicious, and she was used to eating alone, wasn't she? Eating alone. Sleeping alone. *Being* alone.

But that was in her *own* space. A space she chose, an isolation she chose. It was not doing all those things alone in a house where someone else resided. A house that wasn't hers. Without the freedom to do as she pleased.

She blew out a breath and sat up in the gigantic bed. Another change. She had nice sheets back at her cottage, but the bed was a narrow little plank to fit the tiny room. This bed might be twice the size of her bed*room* back in Scotland.

Was she really going to play along with this ridiculous farce? She could walk out of here, call for a taxi or something, and head back to Scotland where she belonged.

But she was all too aware Javier would only follow. Badger, demand, threaten. It was not in Javier's nature to take no for an answer—ever—but most especially when it came to her father's wishes.

She thought of her father now—something she tried to avoid so as not to get mired in the grief of loss that hung around her even all these years later. She'd had a good relationship with him. It had been the two of them for so long after her mother's death, which had happened before Mattie remembered. She hadn't minded going to boarding school as a teenager because she knew her father was doing it *for* her, to give her the training he couldn't. Because she'd never wondered if he loved her, even when they didn't agree on the best course of action.

She hadn't minded him marrying Elena, and by extension bringing Javier into their lives, because the woman and the young man to mentor had made her father happy.

Mattie was not so good as to have not ever felt *some* jealousy toward her father's mentorship of Javier. Or when on their weekly calls when she'd been away at school he would brag on his impressive stepson.

But Ewan Willoughby had been a good man, a good father, with love and wisdom to go around. So while sometimes she'd felt some envy that as a girl—interested in plants and science more than business and money—she could never quite have the same relationship with her father that Javier did, she had never felt Javier, or her father for that matter, didn't deserve the relationship.

In a way, she had a similar experience with Elena. Finally there was a woman in her life to teach her how to do her makeup, or what to say to a boy when he was especially rude that would have him crying to his mother rather than snickering to his friends. It had taken some time, and most of their relationship had developed after her father had died, but still Mattie was grateful for her stepmother.

What she sometimes could not figure was how the warm and giving Elena had raised such a hardheaded son. One who could charm the whole world and never share even a *drop* of it with his mother.

Or her.

No, he'd always treated them as a duty. Not cruelly. Not completely devoid of warmth, but always a responsibility more than…than…family. Even in those years when she'd been on Pietro's arm, running in the same circles as Javier, he had watched her from afar—she'd always *felt* him doing it—but he'd never gone out of his way to engage.

This whole ridiculous scenario was a case in point. She was just an item on his to-do list. A responsibility handed to him by her father.

Mattie scowled at the window. The drapes were drawn so she could not see the night outside, but she wanted to. She wanted to be *outside*. In those gardens Javier seemed to have no care for. They'd just "come with the house." This ridiculous monstrosity for *one* man.

She all but threw herself out of bed. Maybe there was no point going home when Javier would only follow and badger, but there was no reason to be some dutiful little child about the whole endeavor. She was an adult. She got to do as she pleased, and she *pleased* a nighttime tour of the gardens.

She stormed out of her set of rooms and began exploring the dark hallways full of twists and turns and doors. She could remember how to get out of the front of the house, but she wanted to see the back.

One of these doors had to lead outside, but she opened thick door after thick door only to be met with dark rooms. Dens and sitting rooms and empty bedrooms.

Honestly, the size of the place was ridiculous, and she did not know how his tiny staff took care of it.

She moved into another hall, found a promising-looking door. Old and heavy, the kind she would have thought made for an exterior door. But once again as she opened the door her gaze landed on an interior room. A bedroom.

Javier's bedroom, if the scowling man standing next to a giant four-poster bed was anything to go by.

The scowling *shirtless* man. Like he'd been in the middle of taking off his clothes. And she was frozen to the spot— hand on the doorknob, head peeking in. At the impressive ridges of pure muscle, at the odd play of white scars against tan skin, at the fascinating trail of dark hair that disappeared at his pants' waistband.

She could scarcely breathe. Like being caught out in a wild storm, all lightning and wind and icy lashings of rain. Dangerous. She did not understand her internal reaction, but she knew everything in this moment was *dangerous*.

And yet, she didn't run like she should.

Because you are not a coward, and this is nothing.

She cleared her throat, hoping to find some port in the storm inside herself. "I was trying to find a door out to the gardens," she offered, irritated at the squeak in her voice, but glad she hadn't said something worse. Like *Where did you get those scars?*

"Instead you found the door to my bedroom," he replied blandly.

"I'm sorry." And she was, mostly, because as mad as she might find herself with him in the moment, she knew how he guarded his privacy. "I suppose I should be relieved I did not walk in on anything terribly tawdry," she offered, trying to sound worldly and unaffected even as she felt her face grow hot.

"I do not bring women back here," he grumbled, grabbing the button-up he'd had on earlier off his bed and pulling it back on.

His comment caught her off guard considering his bedroom looked like luxury and sin personified, wasted on a man alone. "But it's so lovely."

He looked up from his buttons, his eyes direct. Intense. "And mine."

Yes, he'd always been fiercely protective of what he viewed as his. She should bid him good-night and return to her rooms. *To safety*, something inside her whispered.

Instead she stood there, held immobile by his gaze like some kind of bug pinned to a board, her heart galloping in her chest. Stupidly. When she should excuse herself. When she should escape this thing rioting around inside her like a gale.

"Come," he said, holding out his hand.

Her heart leaped to her throat. She struggled to take a breath and her entire body felt as though it was on fire. Surely he didn't mean...

It was a ridiculous thought. Javier might not be choosy when it came to his many, *many* romantic partners, but he'd certainly never looked at her twice—*and never will*, she told herself fiercely. *And you don't want him to.*

She didn't particularly want to touch him either, but to admit that would be to admit that her mind had gone somewhere it very much shouldn't. So she swallowed down all those jangling feelings she knew better than to have and lifted her chin.

She was no longer the scared little girl who'd been conned into believing a man might love her or care for her. She was an adult now, and she did not let foolish fantasies betray her. Her being anything more than a responsibility to him was neither what she wanted, nor even remotely possible.

She was done believing in the impossible.

So she stepped forward and took his outstretched hand. Hot, large, calloused when she couldn't picture Javier doing physical work, let alone having time for it. But he had scars on his torso, like once upon a time he'd done something other than sit in boardrooms in expensive suits and lead her father's company to soaring profit.

He led her to a pair of doors. With his free hand, he pushed them open and pulled her outside into the dark night. A beautiful balcony stretched out and around to a stone staircase that led down into a moonlit garden straight out of a fairy tale.

The dark earthy scent washed over her, the leaves and flowers whispering those amusing secrets plants had. So beautiful, so surprising, she forgot her hand was in his.

Until he dropped hers, and it felt like a loss. She looked

away from the gardens, back at him, but he jerked his chin toward the staircase. "Enjoy, *cariño*."

She decided that was the only thing to do.

CHAPTER FOUR

JAVIER STEPPED ABRUPTLY away from Matilda. Something…
odd was happening to him, and he needed to find a good
thing to blame it on because it certainly couldn't be *her*.

She walked down the staircase into the moonlit garden
like she had always belonged there, in the warm night and
lush dark. A little spark of flame in a dark he never spent
much time looking at…because it tended to wrap inside him
like feelings, and he didn't see the point in that.

Matilda certainly wasn't afraid to wade in. To show her
enjoyment on her moonlit-gilded face with a bright smile
and wide eyes. She no longer wore the drab brown hiking
clothes, but the baggy pajamas weren't much of an improve-
ment. Though the fabric did look soft…

He didn't realize he'd moved forward until he found himself at the top of the stairs, watching her reach out and trail
her fingers over long, velvet leaves. Such joy over something as simple as plants. The way she touched them like…

Well, it didn't do to think what *like*. It didn't do to think
of her gaze taking a tour of his bare chest when she'd poked
her way into his bedroom.

But why would it not? He knew the effect he had on

women. Why would she be immune? And wary, which was good. For everyone involved.

Such basic…reactions were normal, and nothing new to him when it came to the opposite sex, so why it should sweep through him like some kind of thunder was beyond the telling.

It was just that she had invaded *his* space. *His*. These were his private quarters where no one was allowed. He even limited the staff who entered these doors. Because it was his and his alone.

What had possessed him to invite her to explore the back gardens? While he did not spend much time enjoying them on his own, and thus did not feel quite so possessive of them as he did his bedroom, he did not like how much it looked like this was exactly where she belonged, unwelcome fairy sprite that she was.

He let her walk around, but he stayed put on the balcony. Maybe he tracked her every move with his gaze, but he did not move. When it seemed as if she had inspected every plant for five long minutes apiece, at least, he sighed.

"*Some* of us have early meetings and cannot gallivant around all night. The gardens will not be any different in the morning."

"That is where you're wrong, Javier. They will be entirely different in the morning. Some flowers will bloom in the sunlight, some will droop." It sounded like she was reciting some kind of poem. "A leaf will unfurl. The whispers will change in the heat of day. Everything will be different in the morning."

He did not like how that felt like some sort of dark premonition inside him. Because nothing changed without his permission these days.

"I warned you to get a good night's sleep, did I not?"

She tilted her face up to look at him. He might have believed her some statue of a goddess if her hair did not gleam in the moonlight, if she wasn't dressed so shabbily.

"I am not a child, Javier," she returned. "I know you may view yourself as my jailer of a guardian since you dragged me here against my will, but I am a grown woman."

He wanted to scoff at the idea of *grown*, no matter how possessed and adult she seemed in this moment. But he focused on the reality of their situation—as this was the only important thing. Ever. "What a tragedy you have endured to be brought to a beautiful home with delicious food and have your every need met," he said drily.

Her lips firmed into a scowl. "Every need except the need for independence, freedom, agency." She ticked off all these things on her fingers. Like they were needs, when at best they were wants.

At. Best.

"And," he continued, ignoring her, "I do not recall *dragging* anyone. This penchant for exaggeration does not suit a grown woman."

She let out a little sound then—not quite a laugh, not quite a scoff, but it gave the impression of both. And more… more he could not put his finger on.

Wouldn't.

But she climbed the stairs, with one last wistful look at the garden below. Then she came to stand in front of him on the balcony, rather than scurry off to her room as she should. She stood there before him and said nothing. Just looked at him as though she were looking *into* him. He had to curl his hands into fists at his sides to resist the urge to reach out and touch the burnished flame of her hair.

"I am here." She gestured at his house. The grand house he'd purchased himself. Lived in *himself.* The house that was a symbol of all he controlled, and always would.

"You have won this round," she said, so seriously and with a sadness in her eyes that twisted something painful inside of him—though he refused to name what. Then she plastered on a smile before brushing past him. "We shall see about the rest." She strode inside and out of his bedchamber.

He did not watch the door she quietly closed behind her. He did not stare out at the gardens. He looked down at one fisted hand. *Your father's fists, naturally.*

He shoved this thought away. He would win "the rest" as she called it. For Ewan. For his own pride. And for *her* own good, whether she could see that or not.

But clearly, that was going to require some distance. So he set about to create some.

Mattie was awoken the next morning by a knock on the bedroom door. Disoriented by the big bed, the strange darkness in the *huge* room, and how dead asleep she'd been, she simply lay there for a few moments, blinking and wondering what was a dream and what was real.

Before she could react in any way, the door opened. And a woman Mattie had never laid eyes on once in her life entered. She was all quick, brisk movements.

"Good morning, Ms. Willoughby."

"Uh…good…morning." Mattie pushed herself into a sitting position in the bed, watching as the woman crossed her bedroom and tossed open the curtains and let the daylight in. Which was when Matilda realized just how much light they'd been keeping out. Outside the windows, a bright sunny blue-sky day dawned.

"What time is it?" Mattie asked. She *never* slept this late. "And who...are you?"

"I am Carmen Perez. I will be acting as your assistant for the next six months or until you are married." She eyed Mattie still in bed, a blank expression that didn't do much to hide the woman's disapproval. "Mr. Alatorre has a strict schedule for us to follow the next two days leading up to the ball, so it is time to get up, Ms. Willoughby. It is nearing eight thirty and we have much to do."

Mattie tried to get her brain to engage. Usually she was a morning person, but that was in her cottage in Scotland puttering about *alone*. Not being bossed around by a stranger. "We...do?"

Carmen tapped the screen of her tablet tucked in the crook of her elbow. "You will dress immediately. Then breakfast. We then have some appointments to find you a gown for tomorrow night. We don't have much time."

For a moment, Mattie just sat in her bed and wondered if this was all some very realistic bad dream. From three years of total independence to just...being ordered around. All because of her father's ridiculous will.

No. No, that was not going to work for her. She fixed a smile on her face. "You're just going to stand there while I get dressed?"

"I can step outside if you need privacy, Miss Willoughby." This was said with a clear side of derision.

One Mattie pretended not to notice. "I'm afraid I'll need

a little more privacy than that. I will meet you down at breakfast in thirty minutes."

Carmen's mouth firmed. "We do not have thirty minutes."

"I'm quite certain *I* have as much time as I want."

"That is not the case. Mr. Alatorre has filled your day, and tomorrow as well. The schedule is strict and has no leeway. Perhaps if you'd woken at an acceptable hour..."

Mattie attempted to breathe through the spurt of temper that wanted to explode. She kept the bland smile on her face. Javier had not once discussed a schedule with her. Or an assistant or *any* of this. "If Mr. Alatorre has determined this schedule, then why is he not here?"

"He is a busy man. It is my job to ensure you follow the schedule and are ready for the ball tomorrow, and so I shall."

Mattie supposed it made sense in a way. Javier wasn't going to take her shopping. But why hadn't he warned her? Why wasn't he here making the introductions? Why was he *avoiding* her and flinging this woman at her with no warning?

Mattie didn't know what to make of it, but she knew she didn't like it. And she was hardly going to hop to Javier's— or this stranger's—direction.

"I will meet you at breakfast in fifteen minutes then. But I will not get ready with you standing there watching me or standing outside my door like some kind of guard. I am no one's prisoner, and I will not be treated as such."

Carmen did not roll her eyes, but somehow gave Mattie the impression that's exactly what she'd done. "As you wish, Miss Willoughby," she said coolly. "If you are not downstairs in those fifteen minutes, though, I'm afraid we will be forced to skip breakfast altogether."

"That *would* be a shame," Mattie replied with a smile, but she did not budge from the bed. Just held Carmen's cool gaze. She would not be bullied into Javier's schedule, Javier's plans.

No, she got to have *some* control. If Javier wanted a battle of wills, then so be it.

Finally, Carmen turned and left the room, clearly irritated with Mattie already. Not the best first impression for the woman who was going to act as her assistant for the next few months. But she wasn't really *Mattie's* assistant. She was little more than Javier's hired enforcer.

The thought made Mattie scowl, then hurry out of bed. She pulled on some clothes quickly, knowing time was of the essence.

Because she wasn't following anyone's plan but her own.

Maybe she would go to that ball tomorrow, meet the men Javier wanted her to meet, but she would *not* follow his schedule. She would *not* be ordered around. She would do what *she* wanted to do.

And what she wanted to do was get dirty.

She hurried out of her room, going in the opposite direction Carmen likely would have gone to the dining room. Mattie poked around until she found a side exit, then walked the property enjoying the warm sunshine. Quite a difference from a Highlands morning.

But her walk had a purpose as well. She hunted down the gardener. At first, he was a bit standoffish—until she proved she did in fact know what she was talking about. Eventually, he relented, furnishing her with tools and agree-

ing to a little plot of scraggly plants he'd been set to re-
place today. She discussed the options of potted plants he
had ready for planting and explained what she wanted to
do with the section.

"Mr. Alatorre is quite particular about wanting things
to look very neat. Clean lines. He's not fussy about what
kind of things we plant or how we care for them, but he
does like a uniform look."

"Don't worry, Andrés. I will handle Mr. Alatorre." Mattie flashed him a sunny smile as she finished piling everything she wanted into a wheelbarrow, then left Andrés in the
little gardening building before he had a chance to change
his mind about letting her handle things.

Practically giggling with delight, she pushed the wheelbarrow over to what she was determined was *her* patch of
land. Because she would not be denied gardens for even a
week, let alone six months.

She settled her tools, the pots, then got to work at removing the old and dying plants that needed replaced. It
was a warm day and she worked up a sweat just clearing
the area. When she took a break, she looked back at the
house. She was on the back side of the building, and she
recognized the stairs that curved down to a patio just a little way in front of her. She'd come down those stairs last
night to enjoy Javier's gardens, though she'd gone to the
left rather than the right last night.

But this meant Javier's bedroom balcony was right above
them. It meant if he stood there and looked out in the daylight, he'd have to see *her* progress on this little patch of
land.

He likely wouldn't ever do such a thing, but it gave her

a perverse kind of joy to design a very abstract planting—instead of Mr. Alatorre's preferred "straight lines"—where there was a chance he would have to see them.

She looked back at the patch of soil. No, this wasn't the right space for straight lines and rows at all. It needed something a little wild. Big fat blooms and vibrant, seductive greens. She'd talk to Andrés about adding some kind of arbor. A trellis maybe, with a little bench.

Yes, she was going to make this space all her own for as long as she was here.

She wasn't surprised when Carmen finally found her, though she'd been hoping to be a little further along with her planting when the woman stormed up to her.

"I have been looking everywhere for you, Miss Willoughby. This is *not* what we agreed upon."

"Did we agree upon something? Because all I seem to recall is you ordering me about like Javier Jr."

The woman's pinched face only tightened. They were not starting out on the right foot, which Mattie felt a twinge of guilt over since it wasn't Carmen's fault Javier was an ogre. But still. Lines had to be drawn.

"If you are quite finished, we need to go shopping," Carmen said crisply, her eyes traveling over Mattie's dirty hands in horror. "I have very strict instructions from Mr. Alatorre about what you are allowed to wear tomorrow night, and this is not something that can be put off."

Allowed. This really was getting out of hand.

Mattie shook her head, kept her focus on the plants. "No, Carmen. I'm not finished. Nor do I plan to be any time soon."

"We have a schedule."

"*You* have a schedule. Given to you by Javier. One I was not consulted about, and therefore have no plans to follow. Now, if you'd like to discuss a schedule for tomorrow, with *me*, I'd love to sit down and do just that. Later. Once I'm finished here. But it will be *my* choice, not his."

"*You* are not my boss, Miss Willoughby."

Mattie speared the trowel into the dirt with perhaps more force than necessary as she stood and turned to stare Carmen down. "And you are not mine. Nor is Javier, no matter what he might think or what he might have told you. *I* will have some control over my life."

And somehow, someway, she was going to get that across to *someone* here.

CHAPTER FIVE

JAVIER RETURNED HOME from work earlier than usual in a blazing foul mood he knew he needed to get under control before he faced Matilda. Still, he did not retire to his room or get himself a drink like he should.

He stormed through his estate, having a pretty good idea of where this impossible woman would be.

Carmen's report had *not* been favorable. He knew Matilda had developed this frustrating rebellious streak when it came to him, but he had assumed she would have listened to the commanding Carmen.

Apparently, that had not been the case and now he needed to waste his time lecturing her like an unruly adolescent. When the entire plan was to maintain as much distance as possible.

She was upending *everything*. After he'd been so kind as to give her three years to herself, she couldn't give him six months to get this accomplished?

A kindness, or self-serving?

He ignored that thought as he stormed his way through the house and out the back entrance. Once outside, he followed the sound of humming.

She was kneeling in the dirt, surrounded by tools and

plants and complete disarray. She was dirty and sweaty and looked happy as a clam.

Too many things slammed through him. The fury, dark and potent, had already been there, but something new added an odd cracking fissure of pressure at the center of his chest. A swell of something that felt as though it could take him out at the knees.

All of it wrong. All of it unacceptable.

He fumed at her back, but he knew better than to let that explode. He would not be his father. No matter how many of those instincts lived inside him like ticking time bombs, *he* was in control and always would be.

He kept his voice as bland as he could manage. "Carmen informs me that you delayed your shopping trip."

She didn't look over her shoulder at him, didn't jump in surprise at his appearance, but he did see her spine stiffen. "I was tired."

"Lying doesn't suit you, Matilda."

She looked up from one of the plants she'd just deposited into the dirt. All defiant violet eyes. "Fine. I didn't want to go on a shopping trip I was given absolutely no warning about. I, in fact, refuse to do anything that I'm not consulted about first."

"You were being consulted about what kind of gown you would wear. Now you will not have a say in that either."

She sat back on her heels, looking at him with something that appeared too close to disappointment to be real.

Why should *she* be disappointed in *him*?

"You will go first thing in the morning," he continued. "Carmen will choose the dress and ensure it fits. You will spend your day preparing for the evening's ball and following Carmen's orders."

"And if I don't?"

"I have already explained to you what happens if you do not find a suitable husband."

"Yes, but you did not lay any threats about me spending every second of every day the way *you* want. So I suppose you'll have to come up with a new punishment if you expect me to be your little robot blindly following orders."

She got to her feet, brushing dirt off her knees, shaking her wild hair back behind her shoulders. When she turned to face him, it was in something of a battle stance.

He did not want to battle her or anyone. He wanted things to go as they should.

"You should have been there this morning. *You* should have introduced me to Carmen. *You* should have consulted me about this schedule you want me to follow. I am not your prisoner. I am not a child."

"I know nothing of fashion or gowns, nor do I plan to," he returned, purposefully misunderstanding her.

"I did not say you should have taken me shopping, Javier. I said I should have some say in how my days go, and who assists me. *You're* the one wanting all this to happen. You should have been there."

"I am a busy man, Matilda. Perhaps you recall the responsibility of running your father's company, and the fact that I had to take an entire day out of my responsibilities to collect you from Scotland."

She shook her head. "I am only surprised you didn't send someone else. But I have been thinking on this all day.

Why did you, the man who handles everything so carefully, handle this so badly?"

He could only blink at her. He could not recall the last time anyone had accused him of handling anything remotely badly. And this would have gone perfectly if she did as she was told. Like everyone else in his life did.

"And the only conclusion I can come to is that I think you're afraid."

That at least was amusing enough that he raised a derisive eyebrow. "And what, pray tell, do I have to be afraid of?"

"Me."

For a moment, just a strange split second, he felt as though he'd been pierced through. A bright light shining on all he kept shadowed.

Then she kept talking.

"I honestly can't understand why. Maybe it's because if you have to spend time with me, have to admit I'm flesh and blood, you might have to come to realize how ridiculous this farce is. Maybe somewhere deep, deep down Javier Alatorre is capable of feeling guilt."

"I would not bet on it, *cariño*," he returned darkly.

"Have dinner with me then. Let us sit together and discuss this as adults, without assistants thrown at anyone. Stop foisting me off into empty rooms or onto your staff and deal with *me*."

"I dealt with you last night, did I not?" Which somehow sounded and felt darker and more threatening than it had been. He'd shown her the gardens. The end.

Color bloomed on her cheeks, as though she also felt a dark intent that had not at all been there.

"I am not one of your employees, Javier. I will have some say," she said, recovering admirably. "Carmen can't just sweep in and tell me what to do any more than you can."

It frustrated him that she had a point. Because he wanted to control this and her, but there was no reason for her to simply sit there and take it. She didn't earn a salary. Didn't need his good graces. He wanted her to fall in line because it was easy, but aside from holding her finances over her head, there was no reason for her to capitulate.

It set his teeth on edge. So instead of continuing the argument and risking losing any more of his temper, he turned and walked away without explaining what he was doing. Which maybe was exactly the kind of thing she was talking about, but she did not get to call *all* the shots.

He found the kitchen staff and gave them instructions to bring dinner out to the gardens. Then he returned to her. She'd spent some time tidying up the area, but not herself.

He could tell she was surprised he'd returned. Even more surprised when the kitchen staff brought out the meal and began to set it out on the patio furniture nestled in the curve of the stairway that led up to his bedroom.

"Let us eat dinner then and discuss all the *say* you'd like to have." Because he wasn't afraid of her. Not in the least. If he had any concerns about spending time with her, she wouldn't be here. He wouldn't have fetched her from Scotland himself.

Satisfied with that line of thought, he settled himself at the table while she washed up. She came to sit next to him with dirty knees and wild hair. She'd clearly gotten some sun today—she must have spent most of the day out here.

He turned to survey her work as she filled her plate. The

entire space was filled with small new plants, all different shades of green, a few with tiny blue blooms. He frowned at the lack of lines. The way the plants seemed to cluster together in a mishmash of shapes.

He frowned. "This is not how I like things."

"Well, you are wrong. This will look much better." She looked over at the space of land, and then smiled. A real smile, full of joy and contentment. "Just picture it." Then she went on and painted a picture of what she wanted the space to look like in between exuberant bites of food. Excitement flushed her cheeks as she spoke of trellises and blooms.

He didn't care about plants, but he found himself wanting to know the difference between the two Matilda had been planting. Because she spoke with her hands, broad gestures that gave away her enthusiasm. She smiled, her eyes twinkling as she explained her process.

The way she explained it reminded Javier of planning a business merger. The way she discussed what plants would benefit from each other and which needed more space. More sun. More shade. So many things to consider to make it all work.

She looked over at him, all bright and happy, and it struck him he could not remember ever seeing her this way. Unless he allowed his mind to go back to when she'd been on Pietro's arm.

Which was neither here nor there and certainly not the task at hand. He'd asked her enough questions about plants to get them through dinner before he realized it.

Unacceptable.

He cleared his throat, refocusing on what was important. Which was not her enjoyment, and certainly not her beauty. "While your plans are quite lofty, you will not have the time to redesign my entire gardens. That is why I have a gardening staff."

She frowned at him, all that joy melting off her face and twisting deep inside him like pain. "You forget, Javier, I have lived the life of wealthy socialite before. I should have plenty of time to do whatever I please."

"That was when you had a fiancé on your arm. Now you are in search of one, and your time is mine until that happy occasion."

Any easy contentment was gone now. From both of them. Which was good because this was about business. Not enjoying each other's company.

"You will go shopping first thing in the morning with Carmen. This is nonnegotiable. If you wish to have more say in your schedule after tomorrow's ball, that is between you and Carmen. As long as you see to your duties." He didn't like how much that felt like a compromise, but what did it matter what she did with her days as long as she was prepared for the events that would allow her to meet her future husband?

She studied him for a long moment and then she smiled. In a way he did not trust. "Very well."

He was not sure what was worse. Arguments or easy agreements. Arguing gave him a headache. He didn't trust her acquiescence at all. "You will find an appropriate wardrobe for the next six months. Gowns. Elegant clothes befitting your station. No more of this drab hiking wear."

"Naturally," she agreed, far too easily. She wiped her mouth on a napkin, settled it over her plate.

"*I* am in control here."

Her mouth curved as she stood. "Why Javier, what would make you think otherwise?" Then she sauntered off—*sauntered*, all hips swaying and mature confidence. As though she was yanking and unspooling all of his control.

And he was left staring at a little patch of overturned dirt, little clusters of happy plants tumbling over each other. Not controlled. Not precise.

Ruining everything. Just like her.

Mattie did not want to go shopping. Not alone and certainly not with Carmen, but the next morning she got ready. Not to be dutiful. She had no plans to do that. But she would attend all her appointments.

Even if she had her own plans.

Javier might not admit it—to her, to himself—but he'd compromised last night. He'd eaten with her, discussed what he expected of her, and even asked questions about her garden.

She refused to acknowledge the little fluttering in her chest at the way he'd looked at her. Because it had been brief, and probably in her imagination since the minute their eyes had met his expression had shuttered.

And he'd turned back into business Javier.

Still, she would honor the compromise by making some of her own. She would go dress shopping with Carmen.

But that did not mean she needed to *buy* anything.

They arrived at a beautiful little shop that she remembered from her younger years. When she'd been attending events on Pietro's arm, she had shopped here on her own. Quite happily.

It soured her already precarious mood considerably.

"We've pulled some appropriate choices for tonight's event," Carmen said briskly, gesturing at some shop people as they entered. "The sooner we make a choice, the sooner the gown can be altered to be ready in time."

Mattie was led through the store, into some private, luxury dressing rooms. Had there been a time she'd enjoyed this sort of thing? When she'd been Pietro's little jewel? *Pietro's little fool.*

Carmen gestured toward a shop employee who rolled out a rack of glittering gowns that made Mattie's frown deepen. "We will start wherever you'd like," she said.

"I appreciate the effort, and I'm sure these are all lovely pieces." Mattie attempted a smile at her stern taskmaster. "But I think I'll just wear this tonight," she said, gesturing toward the linen pants and loose T-shirt she wore. "I'd be happy to look at some gardening clothes."

Carmen and the shop woman stared at her, mouths slightly parted. "*Perdón*, miss. What you are wearing is in no way appropriate for a ball."

"I know Javier wants me to get all glittered up for the ball, but I'd rather be comfortable than poked and prodded into a too-tight gown with too much makeup and uncomfortable heels." Memories of a life she'd purposefully left behind. "We can add a necklace, I suppose, but otherwise I think I'm quite comfortable as is."

"Miss," Carmen said, her voice firm if still befuddled. "This is… You cannot wear *pants*."

"Whyever not?" Mattie asked.

"It isn't…done. It's a *ball*. You cannot show up in these… these…*pajamas*. I will not allow it. Nor will Mr. Alatorre."

"Mr. Alatorre is not in charge of me." She refused to let him be. "And this is a nice linen trouser, *not* pajamas."

"Ms. Willoughby, I'm sure we can find a compromise," the shop woman said, her voice a little high as though she was nervous. She eyed Carmen, then Mattie, before offering a bright smile. "Something that makes everyone happy."

I only care about me *being happy*, Mattie wanted to say to the both of them. But that made her feel spoiled and silly, like all those tabloids had once accused her of being. So she had to find some sort of…center of calm. Of *reason*, in this very unreasonable situation.

"Carmen, I realize Javier has asked you to help me in this endeavor, but there is really no point in getting involved. I will handle Javier. I will handle my outfit. I will handle everything."

But Carmen was shaking her head before Mattie even finished. "My job this morning is to procure you a gown, Ms. Willoughby. You can choose to be difficult, of course, but there will be a gown purchased this morning. Whether it is your choice or mine is up to you."

Which was just like Javier and his demands and poked at Mattie's temper. "You could pick out a hundred beautiful gowns, Carmen. *I* will not be anyone's doll. I will not be married off. I *refuse* to be treated like cattle."

"Very well," Carmen said, and her voice was calm and officious, but her eyes were ice. "We will not obtain a gown. You will attend the ball in this getup. And you, and Mr. Alatorre by association, will be a laughingstock. Your picture, in these…*pajamas*…will be splashed across every society page. Of course, you have experience with that so perhaps it is your goal."

Mattie felt the color drain from her face. She hadn't thought about Carmen knowing about the whole Pietro fiasco, but of course the woman did. And clearly knew Mattie's Achilles' heel.

Mattie had no desire to do Javier's bidding, but she had even less desire to be the butt of any more jokes. No more front pages. No, she didn't want to relive *that*.

"*Or*," Carmen said, pointedly, "you can go inside the dressing room and try on what I hand you. You can choose appropriate attire for the ball and find another more reasonable and adult way to express your displeasure over Mr. Alatorre's choices."

Embarrassment slithered through her, the heat filling her cheeks. She had been put neatly in her place, and it seemed she deserved it.

"Do you have a suggestion for a reasonable and adult way to get through to Mr. Alatorre?" Mattie asked through gritted teeth.

Carmen's mouth curved ever so slightly, like she might actually smile. "I would *not* recommend running head-first into a brick wall, miss. You will have to find another way around."

Mattie sighed, knowing Carmen was right. So she allowed herself to be led into a dressing room and then was handed a hanger with a deep purple gown on it.

On an irritable sigh, she set about disrobing and pulling the dress on. Except it wasn't a dress. It was pants. Sort of. The top had all the makings of a strapless ball gown. A deep purple with intricate beading around the sweetheart neckline that then vined down her abdomen to the skirt—which opened to reveal slim-fitting pants.

Carmen barged in without asking. Much like her actual boss, she seemed wholly unconcerned with Mattie's reaction. But Mattie could see this for what it was. A compromise. An *effort*.

And that's what she was after. With this woman. With Javier. With her life. A compromise between what was demanded of her and what she wanted. Maybe the adult thing to do was try to find the best compromise, instead of stamping her foot like a child and being difficult *just* to be difficult.

"Ah, see? *Hermosa*, no?" Carmen fluffed out the skirt, tilted her head back and forth as she studied Mattie. Then nodded. "This will do."

Mattie turned to look at herself in the mirror once more. They *were* pants, and maybe that made the kind of statement she wanted it to even though they were elegant, feminine and with a kind of open skirt that hid the fact they were pants if anyone was looking at her from the back or side. Certainly not an outfit made for embarrassing herself.

Mattie touched a hand to her bare shoulder. "Is there something with straps? A sleeve? I feel…exposed."

Carmen tutted. "You have beautiful shoulders, but we will leave your hair down and it will ease any concerns about modesty." She bustled behind Mattie and undid the clips and hair ties that held her hair back. She artfully fluffed out Mattie's hair, arranged it around her shoulders, and she did feel slightly less exposed even if she didn't like the woman she saw in the mirror.

Because it reminded her of who she'd been when she'd been in love with Pietro. Happy to shine herself up, to glitter like a jewel for all to see. Because back then she'd thought that mattered.

Now she knew better. The glitter just hid lies and emptiness. It warped, and it made a fool out of people.

She would not be anyone's empty jewel ever again.

But Carmen had a point about being a laughingstock. Going full opposite—refusing to dress to suit the situation—wasn't actually proving any point. It was just drawing a different kind of attention.

That was not the goal. The goal was to avoid marriage. She didn't have to dress like she did back home to do that, she supposed. She just had to be herself no matter how she looked. She could *look* as though she fit in, *look* as though she was attempting to accomplish Javier's "duty."

But it didn't mean she actually had to be doing it. No man would want to marry a woman who wanted to live in a cottage in the Highlands. No man Javier introduced her to would be interested in listening to her prattle on about botany. Maybe Javier could find a man to be interested in the outside package, certainly her fortune, but never *her*.

This was going to be a vacation, she reminded herself. Enjoy Spain for a bit before Javier realized she was fully unmarriable.

"Very well. This will do."

Carmen smiled triumphantly—the first time she'd shown an emotion other than disapproval and outright chastisement. "*Perfecta*, Ms. Willoughby. Now, onto shoes."

CHAPTER SIX

JAVIER RETURNED HOME early for the second day in a row and cursed himself for it. But his concentration had been shot. Carmen had not updated him on Matilda's progress, which he assumed was good.

But he needed to be certain.

Because this ball was important. Because he had introductions planned. She could not fail him on this, so he would ensure she wouldn't. He went straight to his rooms rather than deal with Luis or any other staff members. He needed some quiet. Some solitude. Yes. That.

He dropped his briefcase on his bed, loosened his tie, then without thinking the move through walked out onto his balcony. Because it was a pretty day.

Not because he was looking for her.

But there she was. Down in her little patch of dirt. She wore a silly-looking hat the size of Spain itself. He could not see her face, but occasionally, she would turn her head just so and he could catch her profile.

For too long, he simply watched her. He could not imagine anything so simple, so quiet, so *mindful* bringing him the joy it brought her. It made him want to go down there and ask her more questions about her plans, about why clean lines were so wrong, about how plants might complement one another.

He was walking toward the stairs down to her before it occurred to him what he was doing. Losing himself. Forgetting himself. And that could lead nowhere good.

They had a ball to attend, a husband to find for her, so she was once again shirking her responsibilities by being out in the garden instead of getting ready. He would have to go down there and chastise her for this, lecture her once again and—

Carmen stepped into his view. She said a few words to Matilda, who sighed, then began to clean up. Then they disappeared inside together. No doubt to get ready for the ball.

Well, good. It was all…good. And now he had time to respond to a few more emails before he had to get ready himself.

Yes, this was all…fine. The odd restlessness inside of him, the off-kilter feeling, was simply someone invading his space. Ruining his garden. Changing his schedule.

He did not like it. He *hated* it, in fact. But it was six months, and he could endure anything for six months.

He'd endured worse, certainly.

So he got a few more work tasks done, though not with his usual razor-sharp concentration. He dressed for the ball himself, doing everything in a silence that usually calmed him but today made him feel more and more tense.

When he was ready, he headed downstairs, expecting Carmen and Matilda to already be there waiting for him.

They were not. He scowled. He was not used to waiting on people. He was used to making fashionably late appearances to events, of course. But this was when the woman accompanying him was his date. When they were late because they had gotten up to something untoward before the festivities.

He was not used to standing stiffly in the entryway of his own home waiting for a woman who was *not* his date to appear. He did not *wait* on people.

He glanced at his watch once more. If Matilda was trying to get out of this, she would be sorely disappointed.

He would go fetch her now, and if she was not ready, well, then he would change tactics. He'd thought he'd been very kind to arrange balls and events that allowed a low-pressure meeting environment for his chosen suitors. But if she would not behave, he would bring them here. One by one. Uncomfortable dinner after uncomfortable dinner until she chose one.

Yes. Because *he* was in charge. He moved for the stairs, ready to storm his way to her quarters, but stopped short. Because she was there, already halfway down the stairs. A red and purple vision.

He wouldn't call her polished. She seemed as wild as she'd been when he'd seen her back at her cottage. A windy Scottish gale all on her own. But she was not muddy or hidden behind droopy layers of fabric now.

No, this was a sleek storm. Lightning and pelting rain. The fabric of the bodice dipped between her breasts, glittering and vibrant like an arrow determined to showcase the alluring curves of her tall, slender frame. Her hair was down, a riotous mess of curling red, and she wore makeup as smoky and dangerous as this feeling curling in the pit of him.

Her lips were redder than her hair.

His body hardened. An absolute betrayal of all that he was. All Ewan had given him. It was one thing to have the passing thought that she was beautiful, to be *momentarily* affected by the color of her eyes, the radiance of her smile or the way she smelled of plants. It was another to be gripped by something darker.

Too close to need to fathom.

"You are late," he said gruffly, needing something to be an anchor and if it was his own anger, so be it.

She adjusted the satin gloves on her arms. They should be ridiculous, as pointless as they were, but they seemed to draw out the delicate ivory of her skin, making her glow. Like a pearl.

"Carmen said you're always late, so it was of no matter," she replied, fussing with her outfit and not meeting his gaze. "I swear they spent hours on my hair alone."

"You are wearing pants." It was an utterly pointless observation to make aloud, and he could not quite believe such banal words had come out of his own mouth. But it was such a strange little ensemble, one that showed off impossibly long legs, encased in purple fabric though they were.

Her gaze lifted to his, a glowing violet as if the purple of her outfit eradicated all the blue from her eyes. "So are you." She arched a brow, but her mouth curved, which did nothing for the clawing fight against his body's reaction to her. "If you object to my outfit, I can gracefully bow out and let you attend the ball on your own."

He decided everything would be best if he ignored her. Focus. Control. The task at hand. "I have three men to introduce you to this evening," he said, turning and striding for the door without offering his arm.

He would not touch her if he could help it.

"Three?"

"We are playing the odds. Whichever ones you like, we'll arrange another meeting with. We'll discard the ones you don't."

"Discard? Like waste?"

"If that's how you see it," he offered. He would not jump to the bait and argue with her. Not tonight.

"And if I like none of them?"

He held the door open for her, waited for her to step out into the balmy evening before leading her down to the waiting car. "I have three more lined up for Friday's charity gala."

"Quite the meat market."

"You haven't given me much time to work with."

"I suppose it would have been easier for you if I'd just married Pietro so you could wash your hands of me. No matter what he might have done to me, as long as I wasn't your responsibility."

He knew she was poking at him on purpose. It was the kind of jab leveled at him in business all the time—meant to hit where it hurt, meant to make him feel poorly for his behavior. Javier had thought he'd eradicated his need to explode in response, but her accusing him of such a thing when he'd bent over backward to be good to her poked at all he was endeavoring to control.

Fury pumped through him. That rage he kept buried deep because he knew whose rage it was. Knew what would become of him if it won. Who he would become if he let it consume him.

When he turned to look at her, she took a step back, eyes widening in something too close to fear. There was no triumph in frightening her. Only that sick feeling that always twined with anger.

This is who you are, a dark voice whispered.

And he knew it was the truth, but he also knew how to control it. Even if he couldn't seem to control *her*.

When he spoke, he made certain his voice was ice over the fire that must have shown in his expression. "*I* was the one who saved you from that farce with Pietro, Matilda. It would do good to remember it and how much worse it would have been had I not intervened. It would do good to remember that I act *only* in your father's stead. Behaving the spoiled brat does neither of us any favors. I am being beyond reasonable by affording you the chance to choose yourself. By giving you these opportunities to do that which you would not do on your own. *I* have bent over backward to give you the gift of *choice*."

She retook the step she'd retreated from. Now it was anger that flashed in her violet eyes, instead of fear. "You are delusional if you think flinging me at random men and demanding I marry one of them because of some archaic decision my father made is a *choice*."

Javier waved off the driver and opened the back door of the limousine for Matilda himself. He waited until she was close enough that he could speak quietly, in little more than a whisper. "Perhaps I am, *cariño*. But if you find yourself a husband, you can be rid of me and my delusions forever."

And it would be forever.

Once she was married off, he would make certain he never laid eyes on Matilda Willoughby again.

Mattie didn't say anything on the drive to the event. She wanted to be angry. She wanted to be indignant. But she was just getting tired. Tired of conflict. She wanted to go home to Scotland and hide from all this...upheaval.

This morning she'd told herself she was going to be an adult about this. She'd had plans to plaster on a smile, do whatever she liked, and prove to Javier that no one would be interested in her.

Then she'd walked down those stairs expecting some kind of reaction from him. She hadn't fully realized she'd been holding her breath waiting for him to say something. Positive or negative. She'd stood there waiting for *something*.

But he'd only commented on the time, when Carmen had assured her he wouldn't mind being late. He'd commented on her pants, but without approval or disapproval. Then jumped straight into the business at hand.

Wiping his hands of her, no matter how she felt about it. He'd made it abundantly clear—even if he *had* eaten dinner with her last night and asked her what felt like insightful questions about gardening—that he wanted as little to do with her as possible.

And she felt strangely crushed, which made no sense to her. So she'd fallen back into the bad habit of poking at him, seeking that reaction she didn't want, but couldn't seem to stop seeking out. She kept reverting back to a fight.

Maybe that wasn't all that strange. Javier *had* acted as her guardian for the last few years of her schooling. Elena had been the actual parental figure, but it was Javier who'd had the control.

So maybe the rebellion was natural, but she needed to find some kind of maturity in the face of him. He was a formidable opponent in this strange war they found themselves in.

Mattie had to be smarter.

But it was a bit lowering to realize that running off and living an isolated life hadn't actually given her power or maturity, only the illusion of it. For three years, she'd held on to the belief that she'd built herself into a woman she could be proud of.

For the first time, she wondered if that were true. Or if she'd just…run off and hidden. It was her first reaction, even now. Not to find a way to deal with him, but to run away.

When the car came to a stop in front of the event venue, Javier made no move to help her out of the car, or to take her arm as they entered the big, crowded building. He stayed close, but he did not even lay a finger on her. She didn't know why she should notice such a thing. They were not on a date. He was acting as her guardian. But it seemed odd there wasn't even the faintest touch of the elbow to guide her this way or that. She just had to follow him.

The large ballroom was packed with people in tuxes and sparkling gowns. Some people's gazes skipped right over her and landed on Javier—women's eyes in particular. Some people did the kind of double take that made her shoulders tense because she knew she was being recognized from her infamous broken engagement, from the knowledge she'd fallen for a schemer like Pietro.

She wondered in this moment how she'd been thrust back into this world. Surely she should have found a way around Javier's stubbornness back in Scotland. Thrown herself to the ground and demanded he carry her, force her. Maybe instead of maturity, she needed to lean into childishness.

"Ah, here is your Option A," Javier said, his voice low and gravelly in her ear, causing a strange little fissure of electricity to move over her skin.

Nerves, likely. "Is this how we'll refer to them?" Mattie asked, disappointment in herself making her feel tired, her limbs heavy. "I can't wait to see what you have up your sleeve for X, Y and Z."

"His name is Clark Linn," Javier said, ignoring her. "Your father worked with him when he first started at WB and quite liked him."

"Are you setting me up with men old enough to be my father, Javier? I may have issues, but I don't think I have daddy ones."

He sighed. Heavily. "It was an internship while Clark was at university when he worked with your father. Clark is thirty. Is this an acceptable age for you, *cariño*, or would you prefer man-babies?"

Mattie didn't bother to respond to that as Javier led her over to a man leaning against the bar. When he spotted Javier, he straightened and flashed a very white smile.

He was dressed as fashionably as Javier, ruthlessly styled. His shoes gleamed. His blond hair was slicked back without a lock out of place. But something about his polite smile left her feeling…gross.

"Clark Linn," Javier greeted. "Good to see you this evening. I wanted to introduce you to Mr. Willoughby's daughter, Matilda."

Clark held out a hand and enthusiastically shook Mattie's. She noted his other hand didn't let go of the nearly empty glass. "Nice to meet you."

"You as well, Mr. Linn," she greeted with a smile, since it wasn't this man's fault Javier was an unreasonable gargoyle.

"Oh, you'll have to call me Clark or my dad is likely to appear in a puff of dark evil smoke." He laughed heartily at his own joke.

Javier didn't even smile. "If you'll excuse me, I have to speak with Mrs. Alonso. I'll be right back." Javier slipped away and Mattie turned her attention to Clark, trying to dream up something to say.

Something other than *I have no idea why I'm here, why I'm engaging in this farce, or why anyone ever does.*

"I rather enjoy these charitable things," Clark said, gesturing around the ballroom. "Makes you feel like you're making a difference and all that." He took a sip of his drink, looked her up and down quickly before flashing another very white smile. "I'm *very* involved in charity."

"Oh? Which ones?" Mattie asked, standing awkwardly next to the bar. She thought he might suggest they move to a table, or at least out of the way of people trying to get service, but Clark remained parked right there, signaling the bartender to refill his drink.

"Oh, my mother handles the specifics. I'm on the board of one." His eyebrows beetled together. "Something about blind children, I believe? You'd have to ask her."

Mattie tried very hard not to frown. To keep her smile

in place. His *mother*. And Javier had scoffed at younger people being man-babies.

"I'm very busy, you see," he explained. "I'm a senior analyst with WB."

"Naturally."

He blinked at that, as if uncertain that her response was positive or negative. It was decidedly negative, but he shook his head as if shaking the possibility away.

"I knew your father. He was a good man." Clark lifted his refilled drink, took a long sip.

"He was," Mattie agreed. And his *mother* certainly hadn't been in charge of the charities her father had aligned himself with.

"We used to go golfing together when I was interning for him. He'd gone to uni with my father, naturally. But I always beat the son of a..." Clark trailed off, cleared his throat. "Well, you know, he insisted on using these old clubs. I'm very interested in science, of course, so I have state of the art." He started prattling on about golf clubs of all things.

On and on and on. Mattie could only stare at his mouth. No words penetrated. They were too boring. But his lips kept moving and moving and *moving*. Like an animatronic robot.

He hadn't even taken a breath to give her the chance to get a drink for herself—since he didn't offer, though he kept signaling for refills of his own. She'd about kill for a drink right now, but he just kept *going*. Until she thought she was either going to scream or run away.

But that would be embarrassing, for the both of them, so she blurted out the first thing she could think of once he took a pause to take a drink. "Would you like to see a photograph of my garden?" she asked brightly. Because if he could go on and on about *his* passion—even if she didn't understand how anyone could be passionate about *golf clubs*—why couldn't she go on and on about hers?

"Erm. Well, certainly."

"It's back in Scotland. That's where I've spent the past few years. I have a keen interest in botany, so I've done some experiments." She pulled her phone out of her purse and pulled up a picture of her experimental garden back at the cottage. "I used spikenard, it's a native plant to the Highlands. You see, this was the control section." She pointed at the center square. "Then I tested different kinds of fertilizer in these other squares. All on the same plant with the same sun and water."

"Fertilizer," he repeated, as if he couldn't quite believe that's what they were talking about.

And that's what gave her the idea to go in fully, because she certainly hadn't understood why he'd been talking about golf, but he'd gone on and on and on. So now it was time for some golf club payback. "Yes, and there are so many different options to choose from, but much as I anticipated, my experiment showed manure really is the best option."

"I beg your pardon."

"I mean compost, of course, but nothing beats what nature offers of its own accord. Luckily my place in Scotland is near a lot of farms. Now, worm castings are also an interesting option. I had some success there." She smiled up at him, truly enjoying herself and the way he looked like a deer caught in headlights.

It was wrong, probably, but maybe maturity could wait. "Let me tell you about worm castings, Clark."

CHAPTER SEVEN

JAVIER COULD NOT fathom why his gaze kept going back to Matilda, particularly when Valeria Ortega was talking to him, and he knew exactly where that could lead if he let it. A *very* pleasurable evening with absolutely no strings.

His favorite kind.

But she was talking about some beach, and it all felt very superficial when the important goal of tonight was Matilda finding a man she could potentially marry. So she could get out of his house. So she could be out of his orbit forever.

She still talked to Clark, and they hadn't moved from the bar. Clark had not gotten her a drink or invited her to dance, but they seemed to be engaged in a great and deep conversation.

She was *grinning* at that idiot. It awoke something dark and ugly inside him, and he could not fathom why. He ground his teeth together. Clark had seemed like an acceptable option days ago. Javier didn't often second-guess himself, but watching Matilda chat with him, her whole face lighting up with entertainment, seemed to point out all Clark's many faults that Javier had not considered before.

What had once seemed something in common—wealthy families with lots of ties to WB—now seemed to highlight what an ineffectual result of nepotism Clark really was. What Javier had always considered a bland kind of uselessness now seemed like a dangerous brand of ineptitude. When Matilda needed someone...stronger. A man who would take care of her. Who would steer her in the right direction. She did not need to be married off to someone who she would have to play *mother* to.

"I thought she was your ward or some such," Valeria said at his side.

Javier didn't startle, nor did he look at the woman who spoke. Not when Clark was leaning his mouth toward Matilda's ear. "She is," he practically growled.

Matilda had been against this whole thing and now she was cuddling up to Clark Linn of all useless people? This just proved she needed a guardian. If her inner compass was really this off then—

"Then why are you staring after her like a scorned lover?"

Javier whipped his face around to look at the woman. Her eyes widened and she startled back a little, no doubt at the fury on his face.

Like father, like son. In the blood.

Javier took a careful breath and wiped any trace of anger off his face, even though it still leaped and twisted inside him. A mark he'd never be free from.

But he would control that mark. Always. And much better once Matilda was situated. When he spoke, he spoke in a low, bland kind of tone making sure he gave the woman in question a carefully crafted expression of gentle recrimination.

"I can see how you might be confused, but it is my responsibility to ensure Ms. Willoughby's future is taken care of. This is not a responsibility I take lightly."

"Ah, I see."

But it was clear she did not. So Javier made his excuses. Whatever might have happened with Valeria was of no matter anyway. He had crafted the image of a playboy, and sometimes it was easy to *be* that image, but sometimes things took precedence over the mindlessness two people could find in each other.

His focus had to be Matilda, not his baser urges.

It was clear she had no sense when it came to men. She was showing Clark something on her phone, and she looked as happy as he'd seen her in her little garden plot this afternoon.

Javier had to make a conscious effort not to scowl. He plucked a flute of champagne from a passing tray and then made a beeline toward Matilda, ignoring anyone who hailed him along the way.

And he ignored Clark as he approached as well. "You look thirsty," he said to Matilda, handing her the glass.

"Oh." She frowned a little, taken off guard, but took the offered drink. "I am, thank you." She pointed at Clark with her free hand. "I was just telling Clark about my gardens."

"Extensively," Clark muttered into his glass, with another word that sounded alarmingly like *manure*. Then he brightened. "Oh, there's my mother. Excuse me, won't you?" And he beat a hasty retreat.

"Did he say…manure?"

"It's the best fertilizer option in a garden. Particularly when dealing with native plants and Highlands soil." She sipped her drink, then smiled up at him, with such fake innocence he felt the very strangest sensation that he wanted to smile back. Clever, she was that. Always had been, even when she hadn't been able to wield it quite so sharply.

But it was at cross purposes to his goals, so he could not enjoy it. Would not.

"You can try to scare off every suitor, Matilda, but it will not change the necessary actions required of you."

She sighed and rolled her eyes. "Javier, he spoke of nothing but golf clubs. He couldn't even tell me the charity he was on the board for. Talk of manure felt only fair."

Javier hid the wince. For some reason, even though he understood her position, he couldn't quite admit his error. Even as relieved as he felt that she had not been charmed by the likes of Clark Linn. "Your father liked him."

"That just makes me depressed. He's a pompous fool. At *best*. My word. Do *you* like him? Because I'm not sure what's worse. That you enjoy his company and think he's someone I could ever consider marrying, or that you're just flinging me at anyone with a pulse."

"There is nothing wrong with Clark."

"Perhaps not. But I'd rather talk about worm castings than golf. I'd rather talk about the digestive tracts of rats than listen to another man ever discuss his putter." She scowled into her drink that *he* had supplied. "It wasn't even a euphemism."

Javier did not care for the disappointment in her tone, as if she would have preferred the man make crude mention of his…putter.

"Javier, you can't really expect this to work," she said, turning to face him, her violet eyes full of exasperation.

"It was one man, Matilda. I have many more lined up."

Of course, as he went through his mental list, he was wondering why he'd included most of them. They all had something wrong with them, and picturing Matilda laughing with any of them made him feel…off.

Her gaze surveyed the room. "Lucky me," she said darkly.

"The next one is Diego Reyes. He is a controller at the botanical gardens. This should spark your interest, no?" Something in common. That was why he'd chosen Diego. He could give her something she wanted.

Why that felt like acid in his gut he would not consider.

"What on earth is a controller?" she asked, sounding exasperated.

"Finance, *cariño*. He comes from old money here in Barcelona, and while his profession might be dollars and cents, he has an interest in the gardens themselves. He may even care about worm casings."

"Castings," she muttered.

"We will find him and I will introduce you."

"Or I could go home. And I don't mean *your* home."

"Do you really want to be alone in that tiny little cottage forever?" What she really wanted was of no matter, of course, but he did not understand her choices. Her wants. Clearly some people remembered her little stint with fame, but most did not pay her any special mind. Years had passed. She could go back to the heiress life she'd had without much problem.

She'd enjoyed herself back then. How she could go from enjoying that to enjoying a Highlands cottage made no sense.

"I don't know, but I'd rather be alone than be chained

to someone I can't stand. I know you think our parents did not love each other, so I won't argue that point, but I know they enjoyed each other's company."

He had no wish to discuss that. She had been young and naive. *He* had been old enough to understand all their parents had found in each other was comfort. Not love.

Never love.

"So, we wipe Clark off the list," Javier said, focusing on the important task at hand. "And we give Diego the time of day. You cannot expect to find an enjoyable companion when your only companion is plants. If nothing else, I do this for your mental health."

"Oh, yes, of course. You are a selfless saint, Javier. Everyone knows this about you."

No, he did not consider himself selfless, but he did consider himself in charge. Someone who knew what was best for her, as her father would have wished it.

So he hailed Diego from across the room. "Let us move on to bachelor number two."

Diego did in fact have an interest in plants, Mattie found. He even told some entertaining stories about the botanical gardens and made her eager to visit. For a few fleeting moments, she thought maybe... Maybe she could suck it up and do as Javier wanted and maybe in all this ridiculousness, she could find someone who might not be odious.

She had no plans to marry *anyone* in six months' time, but that didn't mean she had to be completely close-minded to the beginnings of a relationship, she supposed. Diego was handsome and charming and they shared a common interest. He didn't even flinch when she mentioned worm castings—she was considering that a sort of litmus test for all these men Javier threw at her.

She glanced around the room, not fully realizing what she was doing until her gaze landed on Javier. He stood—about a head taller than the two other men he spoke with. He was smiling, nodding. He looked...not relaxed, she supposed, but far more...calm than when he was with her. What did that mean?

"What possessed you to wear such a terrible outfit this evening, *querida*?" Diego asked, bringing her attention back to him.

He was aiming that charming smile at her so that the words she thought she'd heard made almost no sense at all. Maybe she'd misunderstood his question.

"I beg your pardon?"

But he reached out, gave the little flare of fabric that began her skirt a derisive tug. "Surely you can do better than this."

She could only blink at him for long ticking seconds. This man was looking at her very nearly adoringly and yet...criticizing her. Her *clothes*?

"You are very amusing," he said, somewhat apologetically, all the while smiling. But there was something in his dark eyes that didn't match the smile as he continued. "But I could not be seen with such inelegant style. The hair alone." He grimaced. "Such a terrible color."

Mattie tried to find words, but she was rendered mute. Flung back into that old place of sheer embarrassment. Mute from criticism. She had never encountered much of it, admittedly, until the broken engagement had been splashed all over the papers and internet—thanks to Pietro.

This was more private than public, and yet she still felt that same awful shame sweep through her. Because she'd thought he was charming for a moment. Because she'd actually thought she might let him take her out on a real date.

And then this.

"I know what Javier's about," Diego said conversationally. "We all know what he's about. Many of us are quite on board with something of an arranged marriage, but I would need to see some effort."

"Effort," Mattie repeated. Dumbly.

"To be seen on *my* arm, I'd need a woman who understood the allure and importance of femininity. A delicate laugh, instead of whatever that thing you trotted out was. Somewhere between a seal and a dolphin. Darker hair, for certain, which can be accomplished in the appropriate salon. Better posture wouldn't hurt. And this *immodesty*," he said, gesturing at her *chest*, "would be ours and ours alone."

He said this like she should nod along, and she almost did. Except it was the stupidest thing she'd ever heard anyone say. It made Clark opining about golf clubs seem like high philosophy.

She dreamed about dumping her entire drink over Diego's head. Or punching him square in the nose, if she had any idea of how to punch and do damage. But something that created a scene would only make this just like the *then* these awful internal feelings reminded her so much of.

She refused to be that girl again. Elena had taught her how to handle rude men. And he *was* being rude, and completely ridiculous. Worse than yammering on about golf clubs.

She carefully set her drink down so she wasn't tempted to throw it at him anymore. Looked him dead in the eye, and calmly delivered her takedown. "Diego, I do not know what you think of me, what you expected from me, but you are a rude, shallow ass, and the idea that I would ever consider marrying you is so ludicrous I cannot imagine how you came up with it. I talked to you as a *favor* to my stepbrother. I think he was worried that you had no friends."

She leaned forward, reached out and patted his arm as his mouth dropped open. "I am *so* sorry you're confused, but I think we're done here." Then she flashed him a smile and carefully turned away, making certain it looked casual and not like a flounce or a storm.

She didn't walk toward Javier. She walked toward the exit. She had to get out of here. Reevaluate what strange twists of fate had led her back to this same awful place she'd left.

You mean ran away from?

But she didn't want that much self-reflection right now. She just wanted *out*. So she didn't head for Javier's car that would be waiting—and wouldn't take her without Javier.

But a rideshare app would.

CHAPTER EIGHT

JAVIER KNEW BETTER than to let his anger simmer. Simmers turned to boiling turned to explosions, but none of his normal calming techniques worked on the drive home.

She had left. *Left*. Without telling him anything. Not where she was going. Not why. This had not been a part of his plans, and it enraged him.

He had never worked so hard to help someone so determined to waste his help. His protection. His guidance. And to be blamed as though it was all his fault when he would have been happy to leave her in Scotland *forever*.

Spoiled heiress did not begin to cover what she was. *Unacceptable* did not begin to describe her behavior. He had not thought he would have to lay down rules like she was still a teenager, but it was clearer and clearer to him that her isolation had not helped her be anything but an ungrateful brat.

He would not accept this. He would exert his control in whatever way was necessary. She *would* be married, if he had to handpick the groom, and force them both down the aisle. If Ewan had wanted something different, he should have lived. He should not have put such stipulations in his will.

Because one thing was for certain. Under no circumstances would Javier himself marry Matilda. He had no wish to marry *ever*, as Ewan no doubt had known and added to his will as incentive.

Javier would not put the stain of his father on another generation, and if anything made that clear to him, it was the white-hot fury that he had been so sure he'd eradicated from his life. Packed it up in a deep, dark box he never let around people.

Only Matilda tested that.

How *dare* she.

A thought that repeated in his head the entire ride home, no matter how many mantras he repeated to himself, no matter how he used the breathing techniques Ewan had taught him. It seemed some twisted poetic justice that the man who'd taught him how to control his temper would have a daughter who would test it with every breath she took.

Javier was practically out of the car before it stopped. He should take his time, find some calm and center, but he did not. He went tearing through his house, determined to...

Something.

He found her in one of his studies—the one he liked best and used only for personal pursuits. No work, nothing stressful. This was his personal oasis.

And she was sitting there in his favorite chair like she *knew*, when she couldn't possibly. She was back in her hideous pajamas, hair piled atop her head, curled up in *his* chair, reading *his* book and sipping *his* brandy.

It wasn't rage, heavy and twisting and impossible to breathe through, inside him, though it should have been. It wasn't anything he recognized squeezing every last atom of air out of him. Just something too big, too uncomfortable.

If he had a scalpel, he would use it on himself this moment, cut his aching chest right down the middle and eradicate whatever this was.

Matilda looked up as if sensing him there. She did not have the good sense to look guilty or apologetic. She went right back to reading his book. "Good evening, Javier," she said casually, as if anything happening was just normal. "I didn't expect you home so early."

"Odd how I felt the need to make a hasty exit when my companion for the evening disappeared."

"I didn't disappear. Your entire staff knew where I was once I arrived home some…" She looked at her watch. "Half hour ago, I suppose. Let's not get dramatic. If I recall, you find such behavior *immature*."

Javier could count the times he'd been shocked into silence on one hand. This was one of those moments. He could find no words.

She had accused him—him, Javier Alatorre, survivor and beyond successful businessman—of being immature. When she was the one who could not follow a simple instruction.

"You knew that I had one more person to introduce you to. You knew that I would not approve of your early departure, and that is why you did not approach my driver. Or *me*. You knew what the expectations were, and you did not meet them, Matilda." He did not growl these words and he considered this a feat of his impressive control.

"What are you going to do about it, Javier? Play daddy?" She rolled her eyes. "Punish me?"

For a moment, it seemed the earth simply tilted. Fire lit from within. A terrible, awful need.

All these years he'd ignored this, hidden it, argued it away as something else, but it had been simmering. And for some reason in this moment, he could no longer deny.

But how could he want her? Why did he want her? It made no earthly sense. Nothing in this moment made any sense and he had to reach out to the wall to hold himself upright. To breathe through too many terrible things battering him.

And she just kept talking.

"News flash, Javier. You do not have the authority to ground me or anything else."

He had not been thinking of grounding when she'd mentioned punishment, but she was moving on—thank goodness. He could too. With careful breathing. With a reminder of all he'd risen from and would not go back to.

"And partly it's my fault for allowing you to steamroll me back at my cottage," she continued. "But tonight made it clear that this needs to end. We need to find a compromise."

Compromise. He did not *do* compromise, but it was enough of a business word he could call on some of his usual cool and calm demeanor when allowing people to think they were getting a compromise when they were getting anything but.

"And what do you suggest?"

"For starters, I will not be flung at man after man at these events. Your taste in men is appalling."

"I suppose that is why I focus on women."

For a moment, he thought she might laugh. He waited for

it, but her mouth only barely curved. Why did it disappoint him to not hear that sound? It shouldn't. He couldn't let it.

"And just what was so wrong with Diego?" he demanded instead, lest he find himself continuing to wait for said laugh.

Something flashed in her eyes, almost like a strange vulnerability, but clearly he was imagining things as it disappeared and she lifted a defiant chin.

"He insulted me."

"Perdón?"

"He said that I had a lot of work to do before he would even consider having a kind of arranged marriage with me." She made a vague waving motion with her hand as if to encompass all she was. "My style was wrong. My hair too bright. My laugh too loud."

A different kind of fury twisted in Javier's chest. Not at Matilda, but *for* Matilda. That anyone would say such outrageous lies to her.

Perhaps her style was different, but it was not wrong. Her hair was gorgeous. Her laugh…

"I'm sorry you had another stag waiting to mount," she continued, not sounding the least bit sorry. "But I simply could not bear another conversation with another insipid… *jobby.*"

"I do not know this word."

"Good."

Javier was tempted to pinch the bridge of his nose as something dull and pounding began in between his eyes. A stress headache, courtesy of Matilda Willoughby. Perfect.

"Perhaps if you wished to be so choosy, you should have not hidden away for three years," he offered, though if

Diego had truly said the things Matilda claimed without any of her worm shenanigans, he was an even bigger fool than Clark.

She shrugged, unbothered. "Perhaps," she agreed readily. Too readily for him to believe it. "And perhaps if you did not have such a warped sense of duty, I would not need to choose. We could go down a million *perhaps* roads, Javier. Oddly enough, they all hinge on your determination to see this through."

"Your father's wishes? Yes, what an ogre I am."

She sighed. Heavily. Which was his go-to, and he frowned at her using it on him. She set the book—*his* book—aside, and the drink—*his* liquor. Then she stood, crossed her arms over her chest and met his gaze.

He wanted to touch her. *Inhale* her and the way she made this room smell like flowers and earth instead of the usual mix of lemon and wax.

He wanted to burn the world down over what she was doing to him, no matter how little he planned on letting himself act on such atrocious impulses.

"It seems as if my worst-case scenario is that you are forced to marry me in six months, and likely ship me back to Scotland so you can live in peace. I'm finding this less and less of an appalling option, Javier. You would make a fine husband as you would not want to spend a moment with me, and I could go back to my old life."

The very idea was like an ice water bath. *Never.* Never would he betray Ewan in such a way, since he knew that could never have been the man's intent. All that was warped within him anywhere near his precious daughter? This was bad enough right here.

And she needed to get it through her thick skull he was not an option, shipping her back to Scotland or no. "Your worst-case scenario is that you marry no one, and I cut you off from everything. There is no *old* life, Matilda. There is only your father's will."

Some of her defiance slumped. "Would you honestly do that to me, Javier? Because that is not the term of my father's will."

"It is if you cannot fall in line. I will ensure it."

She searched his face with too much openness, too much vulnerability showing there in her expression. "I will never understand you, Javier," she said so quietly it was almost a whisper. "How hard you are when it comes to your mother and me."

"You know nothing about my mother, Matilda. You know nothing about me, and it is best we leave it that way. Now, Friday night we will attend a charity gala for the Coalition of Rural Safety. You will attend and not escape early. You will behave yourself as I am the president of the coalition, and your behavior is a direct reflection on me. I will not *introduce* anyone to you if that is the compromise you desire, but you will be required to speak to some men of your own accord."

"Required?" she replied. Then she laughed, but there was no humor in the sound. "What does this charity you're president of do?"

"They help fund and expand rural safe houses, protect domestic violence victims and transition them into new lives. Among other things."

"I'm glad you know the name of the charity, Javier. That

speaks well of you when compared to the awful men you think are suitable to be my husband."

"I am only providing you options, *cariño*. I never said you had to marry either of them. Feel free to find your own." He knew he should not say the next, but it seemed the only way to escape this hideous, inappropriate, inescapable lust. "But we know your track record on that score."

"Yes, we do," she said quietly, that same flash to her eyes that looked too close to hurt to name.

And since he wanted nothing to do with that, he turned on a heel and left.

Mattie sat in the cozy study but only felt a chill. She had known Javier had it in him to be harsh, but she seemed to bring out a meanness in him that made her heart twist.

Her "track record" was appalling. Because it was only Pietro and that had been an unmitigated disaster, and maybe she could admit here in the silence of an unfamiliar room that she wasn't over it. She didn't trust herself.

Oh, it was easy enough to pick out a Clark or a Diego as being a bad fit. But she *had* been charmed by Diego. Then he'd pointed out all her flaws. Easily noting all the things she worried about internally, like he could sense them.

Or like there really *was* something wrong with her. And isn't that what she'd feared? Isn't that why three years of isolation, though lonely, had felt like a reprieve? Because she didn't have to worry if she was all wrong. Whether it be *her*, or her ability to determine if someone was a good person or not.

Funny that she could look at Javier, who was so irritating and overbearing and *rude*, and yet she knew…with no doubts…that he was a good man. Not just because her father had loved him, but because he took his responsibilities seriously. Because Javier had loved her father—for *him*, not his company, or his money, even if he'd ended up with some of both.

It would be easier if she could paint him the evil monster, but she knew at worst he was just misguided. And probably had never really dealt with his grief over her father. He'd probably buried it under work and women.

Women. So many eyes had followed him around the room tonight. And he had smiled at some of them, touched their arms or shoulders. Spoken to them and laughed. He could have any of them, and she could not fathom why that made her stomach hurt.

So she wouldn't spend another minute thinking about it.

She thought about going to bed but knew she'd only stew. She could go walk the gardens, even work on her little plot if she could hunt up some kind of lantern. But as much as those things brought her peace, they didn't eradicate frustrated thinking patterns. They tended to allow her to dig into them.

So, she did what she did when she was back in Scotland and struggling with loneliness. She called her stepmother.

She pulled out her phone and dialed Elena for the first time since she'd arrived in Spain. When her stepmother answered with enthusiasm, Mattie figured she could not possibly know what was going on.

"It is good to hear your voice. How is Barcelona treating you?" Elena asked in her usual warm cheeriness, at total odds with her son's usual icy distance.

So Mattie decided to jump right into it. "Do you know what he's up to?"

"Well." There was a long, drawn-out pause. "Yes."

Mattie's mouth dropped open, even if Elena couldn't see it. Because Elena said nothing else. Offered no commiseration. She was just *silent*. Like she agreed with Javier.

"I know you have your reservations about the situation," Elena said. "But it is not such a bad thing to be taken care of, *mi niña hermosa*. I know Javier is going about it in his typical rigid fashion, but I'm certain you can make the best of it."

"Best of being marched around like goods to be sold?" Mattie could hardly believe Elena would suggest such a thing.

Elena was quiet for a moment. "Mattie, you know I love you. I think you're a beautiful, smart, sweet woman. I also know that you loved your little cottage."

Mattie could not begin to understand where this was going. She just had a feeling of dread settle over her, like bad news was on the horizon. Like this would not be the comfort she'd sought. At all.

"Perhaps this is not the exact situation I would have chosen for you, but I'm glad you're in Barcelona. I'm glad you're not hiding any longer."

"Hiding? I wasn't hiding," Mattie replied, a knee-jerk reaction. "I was *finding* myself."

"I know this is what you told yourself, but… Trust me. A person does not find themselves by refusing to engage with the things that hurt them. I have been trying to slowly encourage you to that realization yourself."

Mattie thought back to the visits she'd had with Elena.

The invitations to stay longer, to move in with her. Suggesting she get another degree, a job. Never as pushy and demanding as her son, but… Yes, she supposed Elena had been urging her toward something.

"I was happy in Scotland."

"Perhaps. Or perhaps you were just comfortable."

Mattie sat a little straighter in the chair she'd been lounging in. Those words hit…hard. "I…" She had no easy argument. She found no words to insist otherwise.

She had been more comfortable than happy, and it was a shock to realize it here. Now. When she didn't want to be *here*.

"Isolation can be a wonderful thing, but it is no good for you when you are hiding. That is not solitude. It is…well, cowardice. I have done such, my dear. It is why I took so long to marry your father. I was afraid of all my past mistakes. All that was wrong with *me*. I was a coward, and it took time and healing to be brave enough to say yes to him."

Mattie frowned a little, wondering what confident and nurturing Elena might have ever doubted herself over. But she supposed it didn't matter. The thing was she'd gotten over it, married her father. "I am glad you did."

"Me too," Elena said, her voice tight with grief. "And I know you are not a coward, Mattie. That is not you. Not at your heart."

Mattie had to swallow the lump in her throat. She felt chastised, though she knew that wasn't Elena's intent. But it was something… It felt like something her father would have said to her. She would have argued with him. Scoffed at how little he understood her.

Then, eventually, realize he was right.

Wasn't this the realization she'd been butting up against in her short time here? She had loved her isolation, but that was because it had been safe. Because she didn't have to worry. She had convinced herself it was honorable, but…

She *had* been hiding. From all her pain. All her doubts. It had *felt* good, but she did not know if it had been good *for* her. As a person. As a mature adult. Perhaps it had even kept her from wonderful things.

Still… Javier's plans did not feel like the right course of action to correct that.

"Do you honestly think I should let Javier take me from event to event, flinging terrible men at me?"

"You must do what I always do when my son thinks he's right about something foolish. Play along. Agree with him whenever and however—externally. Then, do whatever you feel is best regardless. You do not need his approval or agreement."

"And yet *you* think I should go on this ridiculous husband hunt?" Mattie demanded, because regardless of all the mistakes she'd maybe made in hiding away, she was certain this was not what she wanted. "Being married is not the be-all and end-all for me."

Elena sighed audibly in the phone. "Nor should it be, *mi niña*. But being alone is not good for you, no matter how much it feels as though it is. Your father knew you had a tendency to withdraw when faced with…discomfort. And he was right. Perhaps you do not find the man for you on this journey, but you should *try*. Put yourself out there. Allow for possibilities. Possibilities are what life is made of. What is the harm?"

That had been what she'd told herself when she agreed

to go with Javier. *What is the harm*? But she saw it in all the ways it reminded her of three years ago. In the way she couldn't trust herself. It reminded her of all that hurt, and it made her want to…

Well, as Elena had said her father thought. Withdraw. Hide. Because… "I… I really thought I was in love with Pietro, Elena. How could I…put myself out there again knowing how bad I am at this?"

Elena made a considering noise because she was always good at this. Listening, and not responding so quickly, so decisively that Mattie felt honor bound to resist advice. She gave the questions, the concerns space.

"Let me say this. Something I have never shared with you for a wide variety of reasons. Before your father, I survived a terrible marriage. Not because I was forced to marry, but because I fancied myself in love with a man who could not love at all. Not me. Not his child. This was my choice, and a wrong choice I stuck with for far too many years. Then, with your father, I held back. For too many years. Afraid of making the same mistakes when I knew he was nothing like the first man."

Mattie was shocked. She'd never heard Elena mention her previous husband, who Mattie could only guess was Javier's father. Mattie had always known it was not a topic she could broach with either of them. Part of her had always assumed—clearly naively—that he had died, and that the loss was too painful to bear, much like it had been for her father with her own mother. Mattie had never wanted to be the cause of such pain, so she'd never broached the subject with anyone.

But now… So many things fell into place. The scars

on Javier's side. The charity gala he was so serious about. His lack of sympathy for her situation when he'd actually been through some kind of hell, not just an uncomfortable situation.

"I had not yet given myself the chance to heal, to grow, and when I finally did your father was there. You were there. Even this terrible mistake I made for far too long was not the end of my world, my life. You cannot think mistakes are the worst thing that can happen to you, *mi niña*. You must learn to have some grace with yourself."

Mattie closed her eyes. Those words seemed to cut deep even though she didn't feel like she'd been especially hard on herself, kept herself from things she enjoyed because of something she'd chosen.

But maybe...

"I was seventeen when I married this man. And you were just as young when you thought a scheming *actor*—who did all he could to fool you—charmed you, while you were still grieving. Now you are older and wiser. You will make better choices, and some will be mistakes, but that is part of life."

Mattie gripped the phone. She wanted that to be true, but... "Are you so sure?"

"Positive. I married a monster, Mattie. And I stayed for far too long. Your father was a bright light in our lives after much darkness. It is why Javier is so devoted to his memory. Ewan was the only one who did anything right by him."

"Elena. You—"

"No, it is true, much as I hate to admit it. So, do me a favor. Play along. *Try* to find someone. And I will be very surprised if you do not find someone who'll be very good to you by the end of six months. But if you do not, I will stand up for you to Javier, for what little good it will do."

Mattie felt as if she had no choice now. She would do anything for Elena, and perhaps... Perhaps this would be better for her than continuing to hide. Not that she thought she'd find anyone. Just that... Well, she didn't have to fight so hard against it.

But that did not mean she would be *grateful* to Javier. "I hope that doesn't mean I have to be sweet and accommodating to your son."

Elena laughed, low and husky. "Ah, of course not! You must make his life hell, sweet girl. You know, you are not so different. Javier might give the illusion of being in the middle of things, but he is just as withdrawn in the middle of people and business and that haunted estate as you were out in Scotland."

Which Mattie saw for the truth, and it made her heart hurt for him. Especially now that she understood... Elena had called his father a monster, and Elena was not one to exaggerate. His childhood must have been very difficult indeed.

"That being said, I don't think either of you fully understands what a soft spot he has for you, Mattie. He plays the cool, aloof taskmaster, I know, but underneath is still a complicated man with feelings, no matter how little he likes it."

"There is nothing soft about Javier," Mattie muttered.

Elena made another considering sound, but she did not press the topic. "Come now. Tell me about the gardens."

So Mattie settled in and did just that, and when she

went to bed she did not stew or fret or rage. She went to sleep content.

But when she dreamed it was of monsters and little boys with dark eyes and soft hearts.

CHAPTER NINE

JAVIER ATE HIS breakfast alone as he did most mornings. He was relieved when Mattie did not show up to join him but instead slept in or ate in her rooms. The distance and living of two different lives, with the exception of events, was paramount.

Last night had been… An aberration. He was not going to beat himself up for being attracted to her. She was beautiful. Attraction was a bodily function, and while he had no control over its existence, he had every ounce of control over what he would do about it.

Which was *nothing*. He would marry her off—the sooner the better—and never think of her again.

He wasn't totally inflexible, of course. He'd gone back over his list of potential suitors and set into motion even deeper investigations of the men. He'd never intended to fling just *anyone* at her. But originally, he'd only looked at their finances, their press reputation, external things. Now he would know everything about any man who came within Matilda's orbit at his behest.

He would find her a husband no matter the time, effort or cost. And if this unchecked fervor struck him as odd, he merely pushed the wriggle of doubts away.

This was how you won at life.

"Good morning," a cheerful voice greeted.

Javier looked up from his plate and scowled. She was a *scourge*. And not dressed in any of her frumpy, brown, hiking wear. This morning she looked fresh and ready for... well, a trip to the office. A slim black skirt. A frilly top in a color blue that downplayed the violet in her eyes. Her hair was pulled back and ruthlessly styled into some kind of concoction that hid the wild curls.

He did not repeat her greeting, because she'd made his morning—usually spent alone and in silence—decidedly *not* good.

"Are you planning on going into the WB offices today?" she asked, taking a seat at the table. Next to him. When there were plenty of chairs to keep space.

It was of no matter. He focused on his breakfast and finishing it so he could leave. Not an escape. Just a need for solitude. Just *his* life, *his* schedule, *his* rules. As he liked everything.

"Yes," he answered, attacking his omelet.

"I would like to go with you."

He looked up from his plate. "Why?"

"I *do* have a stake in WB. And there are people who were very kind to me after my father's death that I should not have cut off so wholesale after...everything." Emil himself came out of the kitchen and put a plate in front of Mattie. They smiled at each other as Mattie thanked him.

Javier's scowl deepened at the effect she seemed to have on everyone who was supposed to be devoted to him. "What brought all this on?"

"I spoke with your mother last night."

"Is that so? I know my mother couldn't possibly have taken my side on anything, so you'll have to explain."

"She actually did take your side. She said I'd withdrawn and hidden myself away rather than deal with my problems for the past few years." Matilda slathered jam on a piece of toast, but then she lifted her gaze and skewered him with a pointed look. "Much like you."

He should have known his mother would find a way to support *and* betray him at the same exact time. "I do not have any problems."

She took a bite of toast, chewed thoughtfully. She'd put on makeup, and it sparkled around her eyes, brought his gaze to her mouth, the color of raspberries.

"Maybe you don't, but I think it strange. Your mother began bringing you around my father's house...what? Ten-ish years ago? And while we weren't really in each other's orbit until they married, and even then minimally, that's still about a decade of my life I've known you, and your mother, and been under the impression that your father had passed away."

"I beg your pardon." He could not believe she'd just spoken the words. In all these years he'd never had to explicitly state his father was an off-limits topic. He'd thought it clear.

What had his mother done?

"All these years, I'd always assumed he'd died. Not that he was, in your mother's words, a monster."

Ice skittered down his spine. Memories he'd long ago erased threatened to pop out of the ether. He very carefully set his fork down. When he spoke, he made sure his voice did not resemble his father's at all. He was quiet. He was calm. He was control. "I will not, under any circumstances, ever discuss that man with you or anyone else. Do you understand?"

Her eyes were soft, far too soft with too much compassion he didn't want. "I think I do."

"You could *never*."

She nodded. Perhaps the first time in these few cursed days where she didn't argue with him. Didn't try to mount a counterpoint. She just set herself to the task of eating.

Javier was no longer hungry. He got to his feet and strode for the exit, but she spoke before he could fully leave, because of course she did.

"Even if you leave me behind, I'll show up at WB today."

He didn't turn. He didn't even look at her over his shoulder. He stared at the long hallway in front of him.

He wondered if she had any clue the war she was waging inside him. If she would persist in being so *her* if she had any idea where his thoughts continued to dwell no matter how hard he worked to keep her off his mind entirely.

She would run if she knew. Hide. He wished he could let her.

But she needed a husband first.

Mattie didn't bother to attempt to make conversation as they rode to WB's Barcelona headquarters. Javier was angry with her, and for this one, she couldn't blame him.

She thought by addressing his trauma, he might let her in, and that had been so foolish she wondered what was wrong with her. Of course he'd shut her down. He'd shut her down for much less most of their acquaintance.

And still, she could not let it go. What did "monster"

mean to Elena? Had he hurt them? Were those scars Javier had from his own father?

Clearly, he did not wish to speak about it, to share with her about it, and she didn't blame him for that, but she couldn't stop thinking about it. What it meant. The way it changed who he was in her eyes. It gave context to his edges and made her feel like that sheltered heiress the press had painted her. Hadn't it been spoiled and self-centered to never have guessed he might have gone through something terrible?

She sighed and watched as the WB Industries building came into view. It was a strange experience. In Javier's home, or in the grand ballroom last night, she hadn't seen the Barcelona she remembered growing up, but this building had been like a second home.

They'd moved to Barcelona after her mother had died, and she had no recollection of their home in London before. Her entire childhood had been here. And much of it spent in these offices.

The driver pulled to the front and Javier got out. He came around and opened her door, but she could tell the move was grudging and simply so no one who might happen by might witness him being rude.

She followed Javier inside, again without saying a word. It was a strange sensation to be back here, to see so much that was familiar and so much that had changed. To watch as people reacted to Javier in much the same way they had reacted to her father.

Respect and even reverence.

She didn't have to ask anyone to know he was a good boss. She could see it in the way he was treated. And again, this gave more insight into the man he was under all that armor.

What made a good man so closed off? So…hard when he wanted to be? It would be a complex and likely painful answer, and for the first time in her life she wanted to… go down a road of complexity and pain if it meant understanding him.

Javier did not stop to talk to any of the people they passed, but judging from the somewhat surprised looks on people's faces, that was rare. So she had to blame herself for that.

They took the elevator to the floor her father's office had been on all those years ago, and intellectually she *knew* Javier had moved into them a few years back, but she'd never *seen* it, or imagined it.

It settled uncomfortably in her. Yet another sign Elena was right. She hadn't just gone to find herself in the Highlands. She'd withdrawn—away from everything and everyone. And while she had learned *some* things about who she was and gained some newer sense of independence, none of it could really be tested until she left that safe little cottage.

And faced her past.

They stepped off the elevator and a woman Mattie recognized looked up, then back down, then up again in a double take.

"Oh!" The woman's smile brightened, and she hopped to her feet. "My goodness, I wouldn't recognize you but for your hair." She grabbed Mattie by her shoulders, smile wide and eyes bright. "Aren't you a beauty?" Her gaze moved to Javier. "Isn't she a beauty, Mr. Alatorre?"

Javier only grunted and strode for the door to his office.

"Would you like me to rearrange your morning?" Mrs. Fernandez—who had once been her father's administrative assistant—asked after him.

"That won't be necessary. Matilda can entertain herself." Then he strode inside the office.

Mrs. Fernandez shook her head. "Someone is grumpy this morning," she said, with all the opposite cheerfulness. "It is so good to see you. So grown. We have missed seeing you around the offices."

"I never did anything but bother you all," Mattie replied, but with a smile because she had never *felt* like a bother. Her father had created what had felt like a second little family out of his team at WB. "Which I plan to do today. Do you have some time at some point to take me around to anyone who's still here? I... I have been remiss in staying away so long."

"Oh, most of the team is intact. The changeover to Javier was smooth enough, though we all miss your father terribly. Even now, I sometimes show up expecting to see him at his desk. All these years later."

Mattie nodded, a little lump appearing in her throat since she knew that feeling well. She swallowed it away.

Mrs. Fernandez checked her watch. "Give me fifteen minutes, and then we'll make our rounds, yes?"

Mattie nodded. "I'll just wait with Javier." Which he wouldn't appreciate, but part of her felt like she had to see Javier in her father's place to fully accept all these changes.

She stepped through the door, then came to an abrupt stop. So much outside the room had changed, she expected it to feel different in here too.

It didn't. It was still a huge room, with all the same

office furniture her father had chosen. Maybe the carpet had changed, and the computer and phone equipment had modernized certainly, but *so* much was the same she half expected to see her father walk in behind her. To smell the familiar scent of his cologne, hear his raspy voice greet her cheerfully.

There's my Mattie girl.

She fought very hard to blink back tears. Javier stood over the desk, booting up his computer but not taking a seat. He was backlit by a giant window that looked out over Barcelona. Mattie had always loved that view. She wondered if Javier ever turned around and looked out it and made up stories about the people walking below, like she and her father had.

She almost asked him, but then she saw the picture on a bookshelf. The same exact picture in the same exact place her father had kept it. It was the only photo of them all together. On her sweet sixteen.

Her father had died a week later.

"You gave me a necklace," she said. Her voice felt like a throb in her throat, and she shouldn't poke at these old wounds lest she begin crying. But…sometimes the wounds healed better if you gave them a little poke.

Wasn't that Elena's whole point?

Javier looked over at her, then at the picture. "My mother picked it out and put my name on the card," he said, but he did not sound quite as stiff as he had this morning. There was *almost* a hint of warmth in his voice, even if his words weren't warm at all.

She'd known even then Javier hadn't had any part in that necklace, and still part of her had liked to think the gesture had been genuine. Even knowing better. Wasn't that her problem? Blind to the fact someone might not be who she wanted them to be.

The tears in her eyes wouldn't blink away no matter how she tried to fight them. It was too much. The realization these past three years hadn't been what she'd thought, the desperate ache of missing her father, how inadequate she felt in the face of Javier, now understanding that something awful had shaped him.

"You did not have to come here."

She shook her head, meeting Javier's gaze. He looked properly offended at her show of emotion, and that almost made her laugh.

"No, I did." A tear slid over, and she brushed it away quickly. "I had to see it. I didn't think it would hit me quite so hard, but that isn't a bad thing. Some days, I can go almost the entire time without thinking of him. And some days, it hits me so hard out of the blue. How much I miss him. How much I wish he'd had more time."

A little sob escaped, and she was embarrassed, but at the same time, she couldn't lean into that embarrassment. Her father had *died*. She was allowed to cry about that, even all these years later. "But these aren't bad thoughts. That's just the…nature of grief. I'll always love him and wish he was here, and that might hurt, but it's also beautiful."

Then the tears just flowed. She didn't even try to stop it. She needed to get it all out. The grief, the regret. Over everything from then until now. And once she got it out, she'd clean herself up and decide what step to take next.

But for now, she let the release claim her.

She didn't stop when Javier approached. She didn't look

at him, but she didn't cover her face either. She just stood there and let herself cry.

His arms came around her. Warm and strong. In all the years they'd known each other, he'd never done such a thing. If he'd ever witnessed her cry—something that had only ever happened around the funeral—he'd always gone in search of Elena to comfort her.

But today it was him. And she remembered what Elena had said last night, about soft spots for her when she was so sure there were no soft spots at all.

"He would not want you this upset, *cariño mio*," Javier said quietly.

Mattie nodded into Javier's chest. "I know, but I needed to be. For a few moments." She took a deep breath, the worst of it subsiding. She leaned into him, grateful that he was here. If she was back at her cottage, she would have found something to do to distract herself, to disassociate, but there was something far more comforting about standing here in the middle of it, leaning on Javier, as she slowly came down from the emotional upheaval.

When she finally had control of herself, she pulled away. He handed her a handkerchief and she mopped up her face. She took a deep breath, then managed to smile at him. "I know that was probably very hard for you to witness, but it was a good thing for me."

For the longest time, Javier said nothing. He just stood in the exact place, his arm still half outstretched as if he'd never moved it after handing her the handkerchief. When he finally spoke, the words were so quiet she nearly didn't hear them. "I think of him every day."

Mattie nodded. It felt like a strange step *toward* something, even though it was an obvious admission. He was working in his office. How could he not? Her throat threatened to close again. "He would be so proud of all you've done for WB." She looked back out at bustling Barcelona. Those people who could have any lives she could dream up and more.

And she'd hidden away for three whole years. All because some man had fooled her. "I don't think he'd be very proud of me."

"He was proud of you no matter what you did or didn't do. And always certain you would find your way."

"So certain he put forced marriage into his will?"

Javier sighed, but before he could admonish her for yet another complaint about the ridiculous clause, she waved it away.

"It doesn't matter. We don't know why he did it, but we do know—*I* do know he loved us both. So, from here on out, I shall endeavor to give him what he asked."

Javier looked at her suspiciously. "I am going to need that promise in writing."

She laughed, surprised to feel that laugh ease the last little aches in her chest. "I didn't say I'd be *agreeable* about the whole thing. Just that I'd try to do it."

His mouth curved, ever so slightly. A strange warmth unfurled inside her, starting low and spreading out. But before she could really think about what it was, what it meant, his phone rang, and his smile was gone as he moved to answer it.

CHAPTER TEN

JAVIER WENT THROUGH a set of meetings, out of sorts and unfocused. Even in those strange first days after Ewan's unexpected death he had been able to focus on business. On maintaining Ewan's legacy. It had seemed more imperative than anything swirling inside him.

How had Matilda put him so off course in so few days? *Nothing* was going as planned and he could not seem to stop thinking about her. Everything was all her fault, of course, but her crying jag made it hard for him to muster up his animosity.

Clearly, it was not her fault. She was a bit of a mess. He on the other hand…

Matilda's words from this morning came back to him. *She said I'd withdrawn and hidden myself away rather than deal with my problems for the past few years. Much like you.*

Hidden? He scoffed. He was the only one in this family who dealt with the logistics, the reality of the situations in front of him. Every problem that landed on his desk was one he dealt with. He'd been the one to uncover Pietro's lies. He'd been the one to deal with the fallout of the canceled wedding. He'd allowed Matilda the purchase of the cottage, the withdrawal from life. And he'd kept WB going.

When Javier finally made his way back to his office at the end of the workday, he found Matilda in the lobby. She sat, an array of people around her like she was holding court. Ewan's stalwart employees, most of whom had personally helped Javier with the transition to full-time leader, looked at her adoringly. Their little princess.

And the thing was, she sat there, listening to them all, appreciating them all. People who weren't connected to her at all, but who'd worked for her father. Who saw her as an extension of a man who'd been good to them for many years.

He thought of what she'd said about Diego criticizing her, and he could not for the life of him understand what was wrong with the man. She was the most beautiful woman in any room, and while she tested his patience on a moment-by-moment basis, he did not know anyone with as good and sweet a heart as Matilda Willoughby.

Which was why he needed to keep his distance.

Darkness poisoned light.

None of the men he would introduce her to tomorrow night were near good enough. He would have to go back to the drawing board. Find her someone…perfect. As good as her. Or close, anyway.

She laughed at something Mrs. Fernandez said, then glanced up, catching sight of him. She smiled. That warmth, that light.

He needed escape.

Much like you, his mother had said to her.

But escape wasn't because he was a coward, because he

was hiding, it was because he knew better. It was because he was *saving* her. Yet again.

When would any of the women in his life thank him for it?

"If you are not ready to go, I can send the car back for you," he said, not sure why his voice sounded so rough.

"Oh, no. That's all right." She stood, then went around to each person in the room and said something to them, then hugged each of them.

When she walked out of the building with him, she seemed…different. They'd been at odds since he'd picked her up in Scotland, but today every encounter they'd had was something else. She had been sad, happy, determined and in the midst of all those emotions seemingly perfectly at peace.

What must that be like?

"Thank you for letting me tag along today, Javier. I'd like to do it more often, but I want some kind of position. Nothing important. Business and numbers are *not* my thing. But I can hardly just sit around for the next six months waiting for a husband to pop out of the woodwork. I need to do something."

"You are rich as sin, Matilda. You could do whatever you wished. Include sit around."

She shook her head. "No. I want to…participate. Carry my weight. I can deliver the mail or something. Clean offices. Just *something*."

He opened his mouth to argue with her. He could hardly have the daughter of Ewan Willoughby delivering mail, but he understood too well the need to carry weight. "I will see what I can work out."

She nodded and settled back into the car seat. "Good."

"I trust you had a good day then."

"It was like…coming home. Before I went to boarding school, they were like my extended family. And they always kept in touch. When I was going to uni, they were all there for me. Kind to Pietro even when he wasn't particularly friendly to them. They always reached out. And then just because Pietro made a fool out of me, I cut them out of my life." She shook her head. "I never realized how immature and hurtful that was. So busy with my own pain." She shook her head. Then she straightened her shoulders. "But no more."

Javier had to look away from her, out the window as they rode back to his home. He had no desire to catalog all the ways she'd changed in three years, all the ways she was changing right before his eyes.

When change was only ever the enemy. A detriment to the control he wielded over everything.

Except her, something inside him whispered.

Well, soon enough she would be someone else's problem. He'd get straight to work on finding her a suitor she couldn't refuse.

When they arrived in front of his estate, he got out of the car and strode up the front steps to do just that.

But once again, Matilda didn't follow. She stopped under the arbor, lush with purple blooms that reminded him of her eyes. "Your home really is beautiful, Javier. You should take a moment to enjoy it."

He looked back at her, there under the arbor. The sun danced in her hair, teasing out the reddest strands that had worked their way loose over the course of the day. Untamable, just like she was.

Just like this thing inside his chest felt. "And how do you suggest I *enjoy* it?"

She sighed, shaking her head before climbing the stairs. But she did not go inside with him. She took him by the arm.

"Take a breath," she returned. She led him back down the stairs so that they both stood under the twirl and riot of vines and flowers. The sweet smell of the flowers and Matilda herself. She looked up at the arbor and the way the fading sunlight filtered through it.

He could only stare at her. The curve of her mouth, the unruly strands of curls. If their lives were different, there would be no conflict. He would have bedded her already. That detrimental need didn't claw at him now. It twined along his limbs, whispering curses and lies.

You could have her. What would be the harm?

Lies because their lives were *not* different. She was Ewan's daughter, his ward, and too good for the depth of dark in him.

But when she looked up at him, it almost felt as though she shone some light into that void inside. As if opening up to something good, he could somehow make amends of the past. Heal those old scars he'd hidden away. Boxed up. Kept contained and locked away so that they only ever touched his soul. No one else's.

But any light was a fairy tale. Maybe his mother had believed in it. Maybe it had worked out for her aside from Ewan's untimely death.

But she was not related to the monster she'd married.

His father had been Elena's choice, mistake. And this was a stain, yes, but it was not the same.

That monster was Javier's blood. And it wasn't just trauma that made him feel that way. He'd read study upon study of the cycle of violence. Of how hard it was to stop. He understood the science, the psychology of it all. He was marked.

So his only chance at stopping that cycle—something he would do everything in his power to do—was to keep himself apart from any chance at perpetuating it.

And still, they looked at each other, gazes locked, heated. Usually now was the time she looked away, scurried off.

But tonight, she did not.

He could kiss her, in this moment, and he had no doubt she would not stop him. He had no doubt he saw a flare of interest, curiosity in her gaze. This was not a one-sided betrayal of her father's memory. There was a chemistry that sparked between them, brighter with each passing year.

What would be the harm?

It must have been the devil himself who whispered such terrible words in his mind.

But the devil was a devil because temptation was so very hard to resist.

Mattie was breathless. Off-kilter. Something had…changed. In the air around them, in his gaze, inside her.

He was…close. He was…intent. As though his gaze itself was a touch, as if he could see through her. As if he wanted to.

And something that had always seemed…terrifying— his full attention, any harmless touch, breathing too much of his air—seemed less so in this moment where she felt herself changing.

The idea of him as a *man*—not her stepbrother, not her guardian, but a beautiful, intense *man*—was uncomfortable, but not in an awful way. If she breathed passed that initial knee-jerk reaction to flee, to hide from what felt like danger like she always had in the past, to set it all aside, she found herself…curious.

Was it really danger? Or was it just…one of those complicated things she'd been running from for years? *Hiding* from.

She was done running and hiding, so she leaned in instead, though it went against her initial instinct. Though it made her heart scramble in her chest and heat rush to her cheeks. But in the moment of choosing discomfort, she began to realize there was nothing to fear here.

Maybe she'd lose—make one of those mistakes Elena had insisted were part of life. Maybe she'd win—find what was on the other side of this strange new territory. But at least she'd stood her ground for once.

Javier didn't move, but his gaze dipped. From her eyes to her mouth.

Heat shot through her, making it hard to catch a breath. Every sensitive part of her felt heavy, needy. She knew what this was, even if it was foreign. Even if she'd never felt it quite like this with that dangerous edge, with such *force*.

This was desire.

"Some of us have responsibilities, *cariño*," he said, and it came out like a growl even as his expression remained remote. "And cannot spend our day smelling the roses. If you'll excuse me."

"They're not roses, they're bougainvillea," she muttered after his retreating form.

He didn't even pause to acknowledge the correction. He walked away as though she was nothing.

It made her want to…yell. Stomp her feet. But she just stood under the arbor, throbbing, for the first time in her life truly understanding desire. Because she had never felt this wild, dark, thrilling thing with Pietro. He had always been so…kind, gentlemanly. She'd fancied him a romantic because he'd always been so careful with her. Even though they'd dated for two full years before their engagement, he had been clear on waiting to do anything more than kiss her on the lips until they were married.

She had thought it romantic at the time, *safe*. Now she realized it was the words of a man who couldn't muster up the fake interest to want her even though he could muster up acting as though he loved her.

And now that landed in her worse than before, because clearly… No, there was no *clearly* when it came to Javier. She did not know what that moment was. Not *faked* interest—he'd all but run away. So, whatever that moment meant to him, he wanted nothing to do with it.

Perhaps he found her attractive now that she was more age-appropriate, but he did not *like* her. He'd made that clear.

Well, he had comforted her in his office this morning, that little soft spot his mother had mentioned. It was not Javier's natural state to comfort, so he must care in some way. But it was likely only as an extension of her father's wishes.

Which meant he'd never act on anything that arced between them. He'd always see her as Ewan's daughter. Nothing more. Nothing less.

She blew out a frustrated breath. He had looked at her mouth. And oh, how she wanted to know what it would feel like. Javier Alatorre's lips on hers. The thought alone sent a shiver through her in this humid evening air, and for a moment she could almost imagine what it would feel like to have his hands on her bare skin.

This heat, this need that curled inside her was so new and different from anything she'd ever felt. Anything she'd ever *allowed* herself to feel.

Because she always played it so damn safe. Pietro hadn't been, but she'd thought he was because he'd put up a safe front. He hadn't made her conflicted, even if it had all been lies.

Well, she'd give Javier something. He'd never felt safe. It was just now, for the first time, she thought she might want a taste of danger.

He'd never give her that. *Ewan's daughter.* Nothing more. That settled inside her like such a loss she had to… do something. Prove something. *Be* someone more than just a man's daughter.

Well, Javier wasn't the only man in the world, was he? Maybe she'd never felt desire before, but now she had. Now it enveloped her. Other men had fierce dark eyes, harsh, unsmiling mouths. Other men were tall and broad-shouldered and handsome.

She could have desire for someone else. She *would*. At the charity gala, she would find someone who looked at her the way Javier just had, but a man who would *act* on that look. Even if she didn't marry him. Even if he was a terrible person. Even if it was a mistake.

She'd survive.

After all, isn't that what Javier did? Slept with anything pretty that moved?

Friday, someone would want her. And she would want them right back.

CHAPTER ELEVEN

JAVIER FOUND HIMSELF waiting again. He would claim it put him in a foul temper, but he'd already been in one. One that had darkened his door ever since the moment in front of his house two nights ago.

He had been far too close to letting his baser thoughts win, and he had yet to find a way to combat the temptation that was Matilda. Getting her out of his orbit quickly was key, he knew, but it was a delicate situation.

He had to find some better way to…

All thought left his brain as she appeared at the top of his stairs. Siren-red dress. What little of it there was. Acres of pale skin. Her eyes sparkled like jewels, and her hair was loose and wild.

Every part of him tightened, *yearned*. He would burn himself on all that flame, and it would be surely worth it. He nearly reached out for her when she reached the bottom of the stairs. Nearly jerked her to him, to devour her on the spot.

He could. Taste her. Take her. Right here. Right now.

"Is everything all right?" she asked. All innocent-eyed while standing there looking like sin incarnate. There was a high neck to the top, giving an illusion of modesty, but the sparkling fabric displayed her curves as generously as if it was skin itself.

It took great effort to speak. "This is quite a different ensemble than your last."

She looked down at the dress. "Is it? Because there aren't pants?"

"Because there is so much skin, *cariño*. I'm not sure this is an appropriate choice for a charity function."

"Carmen disagreed. She insisted I wear this one. And I saw plenty of women at the ball the other night in dresses much like this one. Besides, if I am to be married, I would want the man to find me attractive. Apparently, some find me *too much*, so I shall endeavor to find someone who does not find red hair and a loud laugh such an abomination. I feel like this ensemble goes with that goal."

Rage twisted along all that desire, so many sharp edges he felt as if he was being attacked from the inside. "If you let that *fool* in your thoughts for more than a second, then I do not know what to tell you. Nothing he said was true. If I had to guess, it was some warped attempt at control. You are better than falling for that."

"Am I?"

"You are older and wiser, Matilda. Behave it. Believe it."

"I shall try." Then she smiled up at him, practically beaming. She linked arms with him and began to walk toward the door. He curled his fingers into his palm to keep from sliding his hand up her bare arm.

"Who do you have in store for me tonight?" she asked cheerfully. Another change from the other night. Her attitude about the whole thing. He should be happy and grateful. Eager to introduce her to the man he had lined up for tonight.

A man he'd investigated extensively. Finances, business. He'd even had his investigator interview people he'd had relationships with—without him or anyone knowing he was doing such or why. There was no hint of scandal. While not everyone had sung his praises, no one had spoken ill of him.

But the idea of introducing her to him when she looked like *this*… "No one."

She stopped and raised an eyebrow. "I don't understand."

He pulled her along to the car. Once they were in the car, she wouldn't be this close. "After the first event's… issues, shall we call them, I did some deeper diving into my potential grooms. I've culled the list."

"And not one person on this culled list will be at this event?"

"No," he lied. Not certain what possessed him. Except… he could not introduce her to anyone when she was looking like this. Like an invitation.

One he couldn't accept. Because in the car was not better. Her perfume settled around him like a spell. Like poison.

"So why are we going?" she asked, turning toward him in the darkened back seat of the car.

Excellent question.

He was tempted to tell the driver to stop right now. So no one but him got to see her looking like a treat to be licked up, savored, enjoyed.

But he was very worried about what he might do if he allowed them to turn back now.

So he lied more. "You said you wanted some say. Take a turn around the room and see if you can't find a man of your own choosing. We can always do something of a background check on him after the fact if you so wish."

"How pathetic," she murmured, leaning back against the seat, looking sad. "Why can't I be normal?"

"Because you're rich, *cariño*. It is a price you pay. It is not something you should take personally. It should simply be something you accept."

"Oh, just accept it? Well, of course. Why did I not think of that?" The sarcasm dripped from her words, but she smiled at him all the same.

He could reach out, slide his hand up the length of her leg. He could lean forward and set his mouth to her neck.

He closed his eyes. *Naturally*, he should want the one thing perfectly and clearly off-limits. No matter how well Ewan had thought of him, under no circumstances would he approve of any of the thoughts Javier was having now.

Her beneath him, naked and his. Taking him deep. *His* for the taking.

So he was a monster after all. But he'd learned how to chain those tendencies. He'd been so sure of it.

Before Matilda.

Mattie would admit, in the privacy of her own mind, that this event was much more enjoyable than the last. Because she *chose* to enjoy it. Or maybe because she had a goal in mind.

Perhaps she wished Javier would have stayed closer to her side since she didn't know very many people. But she was asked to dance by many a man. Offered drinks. She found a woman who'd known her father and had a lovely chat about the coalition, what it did, and how she might be able to volunteer in the future.

It was not so hard to put herself back in the public with a goal in mind. Yes, some looked at her sideways and no doubt whispered about the whole Pietro fiasco, but it had been *three* years. Plenty of the rich and famous had been involved in far more interesting scandals since then.

She was beginning to come to the conclusion that a lot of her anxiety about the public eye was…all in her head. Part of that withdrawing Elena talked about.

"Ah, there you are."

She turned toward an unfamiliar voice from where she stood on a balcony looking over a large garden she'd been considering exploring. After all, she might be determined to meet a man, but she still loved a garden.

She smiled politely at the approaching form, but she didn't recognize the man who'd come up to her. Should she recognize him? "Oh. Hello," she offered, racking her brain for some memory of who he might be.

"You don't know me," he assured her. He was a nice-looking man. His suit fit him perfectly and was clearly expensive. He had pretty blue eyes and his blond hair was a bit shaggy but styled well. He was tall, broad-shouldered. Handsome enough.

"I think your stepbrother had plans to introduce us this evening, but he seems to be avoiding me," the man said, and he held out his hand. "Well, he's busy ensuring the coalition gets all the donations it needs."

Matilda's brows drew together, and she looked past the open doors of the balcony and searched the interior room for Javier. He had said there was no one to meet tonight, but maybe he hadn't realized this man would be here. There must have been some crossed communications somewhere along the way.

She spotted Javier in a crowd of people. There was a woman dressed *far* more scantily than Mattie herself, considering this woman's skirt was just as brief but the neckline was a deep vee showing off generous breasts. All but *smooshed* into Javier's side. His hand was on the small of her back. He had that charming smile on his face and looked perfectly relaxed. She hadn't seen that relaxed posture from him the whole time she'd been in Spain.

She didn't know why that hurt.

So she looked back at the man and took his offered hand and shook, offering him her best flirtatious smile. He was handsome. Maybe she could cozy right on up to *him*. "Matilda Willoughby. But call me Mattie. Please."

"Vance Connor."

"You're not from Spain."

Vance smiled. "No. London born and bred. I moved here to work at WB a few years ago, then moved away from corporate finance and into helping those less fortunate."

"Oh, do you work for the coalition?" Mattie asked. She knew working for a charity didn't mean he *had* to be a good person, but she wasn't worried about his personhood, was she? She was worried about finding some heat. Some release.

"I meant artists." He said it deadpan for a moment, then his mouth curved into a charming smile when she'd only blinked. "A joke, I'm afraid. A bad one. I work for the art museum here in Barcelona in the finance department."

"Well, clearly I have a terrible sense of humor, because that *is* funny."

The blue of his eyes deepened. "Well, we'll have to work on that. Can I get you something from the bar?"

Unlike Clark from the other night, he did just that. Got her a drink, found her a seat. They talked. Of WB. London and Barcelona. He even spoke of some volunteer work he'd done for the coalition—organizing some of their finances.

She mentioned her gardens, and he had good questions if not much knowledge. Which felt fair since when they talked of the art at the museum where he worked, he clearly had much knowledge and interest in art and her very little.

He asked her to dance. He was very gentlemanly. No wandering hands. He danced well, smelled nice and of expensive cologne. He gave her his full attention.

She tried to give him hers, but occasionally she found her gaze wandering to find Javier in the crowd. That woman always at his side. Which would cause Mattie to double her efforts to pay attention to Vance.

It managed to feel a bit like a first date, a good one. She did not feel that same punch she had under the arbor with Javier, but she didn't know this man as well. Perhaps her lack of reaction stemmed from those old fears about being tricked. Just because she wasn't hot all over didn't mean a kiss wouldn't be enjoyable.

"Since you're such a fan of plants, why don't we go take a tour of the gardens?" Vance said after their second dance. He offered an elbow. "I can show you around, and maybe you can teach me something about flowers." For the briefest moment, his gaze toured her body. Almost unrecognizable. Not slimy. More an expression of interest she could accept or refuse.

She tried desperately to have some semblance of the reaction she'd had when Javier's gaze had dropped to her mouth.

And failed.

But she took his arm and let him lead her out to the garden, because there was a chance here to do what she wanted. She would power through. If Vance tried to kiss her, she would *enthusiastically* kiss him back. She would make it very clear she was up for anything tonight.

She wouldn't worry about marriage or forever. She wouldn't worry about if he was as nice as he seemed or a hidden scammer. She wouldn't think of Javier at all.

She would focus on lust. Doing something she'd never done before. Jump into whatever danger she could find.

Because she was done running.

Or she'd thought she was.

"Matilda," a dark voice said from the shadows behind her, and *that* voice sent all that sparkling heat cascading through her veins. She turned to find Javier standing behind them, something edgy and sharp in his expression.

"I'm afraid we must take our leave."

"Is everything okay?" she asked. Had Elena had some kind of accident? Maybe there was a fire somewhere.

But he stepped forward, his expression cold. And focused on her arm tucked into Vance's.

Luckily, Vance did not drop her arm. He smiled genially at Javier. "I can bring Mattie home later if she'd like, if you've pressing business, Mr. Alatorre."

"No," Javier said firmly, before Mattie could speak for herself. "I'm afraid I'll need to take Matilda with me."

"Why?" Mattie demanded, a sinking feeling in her chest that this was not something *bad*, it was Javier…being over-protective.

"The car is waiting."

Which did not answer her question. She did not under-stand what he was doing.

"I'll get your number from Javier's assistant and call you," Vance said quietly in her ear. "How does that sound?"

She nodded and smiled up to him. "I'd like that," she said. He gave her arm a gentle squeeze before releasing her, and she stepped forward toward Javier.

His expression was inscrutable, but there was something in his eyes that reminded her of depictions of hell—flames and tortured souls. And it was something about the thought of him being tortured that had her finally moving, follow-ing him through the gala, offering goodbyes to people with fake smiles until they reached his car and got inside.

She didn't say anything at first as the car began its trek back to Javier's estate. She suddenly felt…tired. "Why are we leaving, Javier? What could possibly be so important? When if I recall you chastised me about not leaving early."

"I saved you from something embarrassing again. There is only one reason a man walks around a dark garden with a woman."

Mattie blinked. He could not be serious. He could not be…stopping this. When she'd made a very conscious de-cision to do…something. And now here he was? Playing overbearing guardian?

It made no earthly sense, and any exhaustion fled as

anger took its place. "Yes, Javier, why do you think I was there?"

If possible, his expression got harder. "Well, I thought you had better sense than to whore about on public property. In the midst of a busy *charitable* gala. Silly me."

The words nearly sucked the very breath out of her, but the sheer hypocrisy of what was happening was too great to be bowled over by. She had to defend herself. "Because you've never done such a thing? Were the women you deigned to touch whoring about, Javier? What about the woman shoving her breasts at you in the *middle* of the party?"

"I beg your pardon."

"I deserve to have my fun too."

"You should have had it before this deadline then. But you chose to have isolation instead. I've half a mind to send you back to Scotland and pick your future husband myself and march you down the aisle in a damn mask."

She laughed. Bitterly. "You might be the most delusional man on the planet," she said. Why had she gone with him? At some point, she needed to find a way to stand up for herself.

She remembered Elena's advice. Go along with him in word, but not in deed. So, she would find Vance's phone number herself. She would call him tomorrow and set up a date.

If Javier had a problem with that, well… It didn't matter. He wanted her to find a husband at all costs. Why should he get in the way when she was finally getting along with someone? Even if her purpose was not marriage, Javier didn't know that.

The car pulled to a stop in front of Javier's estate. He got out, and this time did not open the door for her. It was a petty little slap, and she didn't know why it made her want to laugh. Maybe it was just the knowledge he was angry with her.

But *why*? It made no sense. As far as he knew, she was doing just what he asked. Trying to find herself a husband.

She got out of the car. "Explain this to me," she called after him. "Explain what the hell we're doing, because I am in the dark."

He stopped there at the foot of the stairs, underneath the pretty arbor with all its riotous blooms. He kept his back to her, but he was framed so perfectly by the exterior lights and the flowers. She felt a deep ache and pain in the center of her chest, because…

This was the man she wanted, and she didn't know what to do about it, how to make that happen. It all seemed so impossible.

"You don't find a husband by making poor decisions in a public place."

"Taking a walk is a poor decision?"

He turned then, his expression all patronizing. "If you truly believe that's all he was after, you have much to learn."

"Maybe I wanted what he was after."

"You do not know him."

"Did you know the woman you had your hands all over?" she demanded, stalking toward him. "Because Vance and I *talked*. We had a normal first date conversation, and he seemed to be under the impression that *you* had meant to set us up anyway. So I can't fathom why you'd stop it."

"This is not about me."

She laughed. Bitterly. She wanted to...to...poke him. Shove him. *Do* something to him. But he stood there, stiff and unmovable, looking down at her with anger in his eyes. The sweet smell of bougainvillea washed over her. The blooms seemed to sparkle silver in the moonlight.

And then there was him. Tall. Impressive. Angry, but that only seemed to stir something within her it shouldn't. Why did he have to be so handsome? Why did he have to make her feel like it didn't matter what he said, or did, as long as he looked at her in that way—all heat and need. Maybe that wasn't what *he* felt, but that's what his expression made *her* feel.

"Fine. You are not my prisoner," he said, his voice low, shivering through her like some kind of caress. "If you are so determined to behave recklessly, have the car take you back. Spread your legs for whomever you choose."

She did not understand why in the midst of this ridiculous argument, when she didn't even like him very much right now, her body's response seemed to be: *I choose you*. That she wanted to lean into him instead of slap him or storm away.

His dark gaze dipping again, to her mouth, her breasts. Like he couldn't help himself, because he turned on a heel. "Good night," he said.

Through gritted teeth. With harsh strides. Like a man who could not admit to himself he was running, but, *oh*, he was running.

From her. From what he felt. From this heat.

Because he felt it too.

CHAPTER TWELVE

JAVIER KNEW HE was out of control. He knew all the signs. It was why he removed himself from Matilda and went into his home gym. He punished his body for every last thought he'd had of Matilda, until he was slick with sweat, his muscles quivering and spent.

And still he was hard. For her.

This was an abomination of so many things, and yet he could not control it. Any more than he could seem to control his reaction to her in that garden.

She had been ready to throw herself at some stranger. In the middle of the gala. She might be doing such at this very moment. Letting Vance Connor put his hands on her. Kiss her. Make her inhale with that little shake that made it so clear she was affected by the heat between them.

And he could admit it was hypocritical to have engaged in the exact same sort of behavior before and find fault with her for wanting to engage in it now.

Then a hypocrite he was. He had found nothing wrong with Vance Connor, had been certain he would introduce them, and that Vance would be a very strong possibility for Matilda's future husband.

But this was not about Vance.

It was about Matilda. In that dress. The way she'd smiled at Mrs. Fernandez. The way she spoke about his mother. The way she petted plants like they were puppies. It was about visualizing—very much against his will—what she might have done with Vance Connor in that garden.

It all sent him into a fury he could not control when he had learned to control *everything*.

But he'd left her outside to go track Vance down rather than insist she stay safe in her room. It should *feel* like control, but it didn't. The only thing that he could think would soothe this savage fury inside of him was his hands on her skin.

An abomination.

The workout did nothing to ease the tensions inside him. The riot of emotions he labeled fury even if they were more complicated than simply anger. He stormed to his bathroom and wrenched the shower on. Cold as it would go.

And still, his body ached for simple release.

The water was icy, pounding down, but nothing could erase the heat coursing through him. Hard, heavy. Painful. Something must be done, so he took himself in his own hand. He told himself not to picture Matilda.

He failed. The wild flame of her hair. The way her eyes deepened when she was angry. That earthy scent that seemed to follow her wherever she went like she was some wildflower plucked from her beloved gardens.

He wanted her mouth on him. He wanted to sink into her. To touch that velvet ivory of her skin, to make her scream with pleasure, pulsing around him and—

He heard the creak of a door. *His* door opening. He froze. Surely...

"Javier, we need to talk," she called. As if she didn't know she was walking into his bathroom. She peeked her head in, her gaze landing on him behind the glass of his shower.

He didn't move, didn't take his hand away from what he was doing. For a moment, he was frozen, too many things fighting in his brain to react.

He had not felt such a way in many, many years. He wanted to rage for that alone, but she just stood there. Her cheeks red, her eyes wide. She was still wearing the dress from the gala, but she was barefoot, and she'd washed her face clear of the makeup.

But she did not flee. She stared at him, and there was no doubt she could see *all* of him, what he was doing. And still she stood there, eyes wide and locked on where his hand wrapped around his thick shaft.

It was wrong. He knew this, in his bones, and yet the need roared in his head eradicating all reasonable thought. To order her away. To stop this madness. It could not go on.

But the madness won, the need, the monster inside. So he watched her, and stroked himself, just to see what her reaction would be.

She did not look away. Her breath caught and she stepped closer, her cheeks pink and her mouth hanging just a little open. Then stopped as if she hadn't meant to move at all, as if she didn't know what to do.

"Close the door, Matilda," he ordered through gritted teeth. But he didn't specify which side of it she should be on, and perhaps that was his mistake.

Or his goal.

* * *

Mattie tried to find some grip on reality. She'd been so angry, so determined to actually say her piece that she'd been determined to find him at any cost. Even barging in on his shower. At least *there* he couldn't run away from her.

She hadn't expected to *see* anything, or maybe she just hadn't thought at all. She had just known he'd have to face her. Deal with her.

The air was thick with moisture, the room oddly cold, and she could see him through the paned glass of his expansive shower. There was no steam as there should have been if he was taking a hot shower.

Water pounded down on him, rivulets sliding down his impressive, muscled form. But it wasn't the bulge of his arms, the size of his quadriceps, the smattering of hair over his body. No, she couldn't take in any of that. Because he held the hard, thick length of him in his own hand as if he'd been....

Then he slid his hand down it, and up again until everything inside her was flame. He *had* been. She was shaking, wanting. She *throbbed*. Every inch of her body. A need building higher the longer she stood here, watching him touch himself.

Everything about why she was here forgotten. There was only him.

"Close the door, Matilda," he ordered.

And without thinking, she pulled the door closed behind her. Her heart was beating so hard, she could barely hear the pounding of the water.

But she heard him, clear as day.

"You have three choices, Matilda." His voice was low,

sharp, demanding. It skittered over her skin wreaking havoc and goose bumps. Choices?

She did not feel a choice at all. She only felt the desperate need to watch him. To see where this led. To hear his voice say her name in that dark, delicious rasp that was so new to them.

"You may run away, as you should."

No. No. No more running away. On this, she was clear. Since she couldn't find her voice, she shook her head.

His gaze seemed to darken there, even shrouded by the rivulets of water and glass separating them. "You may watch."

She let out a shaky exhale. His voice was dark, lulling. *Watch*. Watch…what exactly? Everything? Would he…?

"Or you may disrobe and join me."

She felt as though she'd run a marathon and she couldn't catch her breath. She couldn't find solid ground.

She wanted to touch him. She wanted to *taste* him. All those wants she couldn't quite muster with Vance back at the gala were here, alive and bright. And this was what she'd been after tonight, right?

Lust. Maybe it was dangerous to mix Javier and something so fleeting. Maybe it was wrong on a hundred different levels.

But he was the source of it all.

She had never felt this before. Never *wanted* danger before. Now she could not think for wanting it. She couldn't turn back. She was intrigued by the idea of watching him, but it left a strange little cocoon of safety, and she couldn't allow herself that any longer.

It was time she learned how to weather disaster.

She reached behind her back and pulled the zipper of her dress down. She watched his hand tighten on the hard length of him, and it was if he squeezed her deep inside.

She let the dress fall to the floor. So that she was only in her bra and underwear. Such a strange sensation with Javier's dark eyes intent on her. He had not changed positions at all. He could have been a statue.

If she did not see the way his breath sawed in and out of his chest, she might have believed it.

"The rest," he ordered.

She had never been naked in front of anyone. Not like this. Not *for* this. She had never wanted to be, and she supposed that was why she obeyed. For the first time, she wanted. And Javier wanted her too.

That was why he'd stopped her and brought her home tonight. Maybe he hadn't planned on acting on his wants, but he hadn't wanted her to do anything with Vance either. Jealousy. Possessiveness. Whatever it was, it streaked through her like heat and gave her the confidence to get completely naked.

In front of Javier. Whose beautiful form was naked and wet inside the shower. The impressive muscles, the faded old scars that must have come from childhood trauma. The man she'd told herself she hated.

But she did not hate him in his moment. No. She wanted him. All of him. First or last, it did not matter if he solved this aching need inside her.

He opened the shower door.

Mattie licked her lips, swallowed and then called on all her bravado to step forward and into the shower with Javier.

She squeaked at the ice-cold spray, wondering who

would do such a thing to themselves. But he turned her so that it was him taking the icy punishment of the water. He pressed her to the cold wall with one hand on her shoulder, then reached back with the other and flicked the water to hot.

Then their eyes met. She was shivering for so many reasons, the cold probably the least of them.

"This is a mistake," he growled.

"I don't care." Because she didn't. She'd make this mistake a hundred million times if she got to know what was on the other side of all this want. All this *feeling*. Because she was done being afraid.

His gaze slid down the length of her body, slow and intent. She wanted it to be his hands, but for long, ticking moments he just looked. So she looked right back. All that muscle, all that control.

He reached and dragged his thumb across the underside of her breast.

She whimpered. From so little. From so much.

"You should not have chosen this, *cariño mío*. You should have run away."

"I'm done running away." And to prove it, she leaned forward. She pushed off the wall and onto her tiptoes, crashing her mouth to his and flinging her arms around his wet shoulders with more desperation than grace.

Then he was kissing her. Finally. It felt like she'd been waiting for this for *years*, when it had only been days since she'd finally begun to accept that she was attracted to him. That she might be curious to see where the heat in his gaze led.

Naked. Wet. Aching, deep inside. His hands molded over

her curves. Big, hot. His mouth devoured hers, tongue and teeth and a need so sharp she didn't know how much more she could stand before she burst.

She needed something. So much. "Please," she said, even though she wasn't quite sure what she begged for. Only something more.

And he gave it to her, his large hand sliding between her legs.

Where no one else had ever been, and somehow, someway, it felt exactly right that it should be him. For all his sternness, the way he blocked himself off, she trusted him. Always had, even when she'd been afraid of what she'd felt.

He touched her there, expert fingers gliding her toward some new plane of existence. All heat and joy. She moved shamelessly against his hand. She would have done anything to chase the feeling he was giving her.

"Greedy," he murmured. "My greedy little flame. Look at you. Wet and desperate. Lose yourself, Matilda. Lose yourself on my fingers."

It was his dark voice, the twist of his fingers, the hot water spraying around them. It was all of it that had her exploding over some new edge, some new world. Into a storm made up only of sensation and the dark, dark heat of Javier's eyes.

She shook, nearly lost her footing, but he held her upright. Held her there as she tried to find some internal balance when everything inside her had shifted, changed, brightened into something different than she'd ever expected.

Had it always been him? She'd convinced herself he was dangerous, something to withdraw from, but maybe all along she'd known this existed on the other side of her fear. And she hadn't been ready for it.

Until now.

His hands moved over her, up her abdomen and over her breasts, his gaze following along until one hand slid up her throat, then stayed there, as if he needed to pin her in place when he only needed that fierce dark gaze to do that.

She did not know why it felt like her entire life centered there on his hand. She did not know why this storm raged inside her when the move should feel threatening.

But it didn't.

It felt like her power up against his.

And she was winning, because he was giving her what she wanted. Almost. *Almost.* "Javier. Please."

"What is it you beg for, *cariño mío*?" he murmured, his palm at her throat, his thumb and forefinger tracing the line of her jaw.

She didn't have much more than the simplest words for this act she'd never done. Never felt the need to. Until him. "You. Inside me."

The noise he made was nearly feral, all growl and wild. He lifted her leg, opening her for him. Lifting her to the exact height she needed to be to take him deep within.

And then he was inside her. So big, too big. Not painful so much as a weight she couldn't make space for, couldn't accommodate, though she wriggled in place to attempt to do just that. To find something other than this great stretching.

She sucked in a breath, let it slowly out. His groan rumbled through her, a riot of sparks. His chest brushed against her taut nipples, and she arched, pressed, slowly accepted all that length.

The water pounded around them, the air heavy with moisture, and Javier Alatorre was inside her, holding her there. His eyes fierce, his grip tight, and then he moved. All that *too much* shifted into a need for more. Much more. All the more.

They moved together in some dance she'd never been taught but it felt familiar all the same. As if this had always existed inside her. Inside *them*. Tension twisted, built. So many sensations overwhelming her. Hot water, coarse hair, slick skin.

Until it was impossible, this height to which he'd taken her. So high, so achingly wondrous she cried out as it all crashed over, wave after wave. It rattled through her. Not just a storm, but an entire cataclysmic event, because she could feel him shudder as he thrust deep one last time. She could *feel* that he hadn't just brought her to some mind-melting state, she'd brought him there too.

His breathing was rapid, and she could feel tension slowly come back into his body. "This means nothing," he said darkly, all foreboding promise. "It will never happen again. *Never*."

His words were harsh, ragged. *Desperate*. Because he had to know. He'd changed her, inside and out. Bright and new and his.

His.

No matter what he said about *never*.

CHAPTER THIRTEEN

THE REASONABLE THING to do would be to send her on her way. Javier had made himself a promise there, deep inside her beautiful form.

Only once. Never again. Not his. Just the release of a pressure valve so they could go on through the rest of the next few months by putting this behind him. It was better this way. No wondering would haunt them, tempt them, destroy them. Now they knew.

He wished he'd never discovered that sex, something he had always quite enjoyed, could be different. Could be less about the brief hit of pleasurable dopamine and more about the entire experience.

About the woman, so beautiful, so open, so very much his.

No. Not *his*. That was the whole point. He'd put his hands all over Ewan's perfect daughter and now he had to atone for such a mistake. A onetime mistake.

They would need a businesslike distance to move forward. But first she was standing in his shower, dripping wet and shaking from release. That needed to be taken care of. He turned off the water, retrieved two towels. He tied one around his waist and bundled her up in the other and carried her to bed.

Where he never allowed anyone. *His* space. *His* world.

It should have been unfathomable, but he laid her down in the middle of the large mattress and knew, deep in places he didn't like to look, she was exactly where she was meant to be.

She stretched out on his bed, eyes closed, wrapped in the white towel, her red hair darker wet. She sighed, all sated contentment. And he knew how he *should* feel: horrified, repentant, guilty and damned.

But no matter what he knew, he could not seem to work up those feelings. Not when she looked so happy. Nothing dark and heavy slithered through him. He felt light and…

Things he couldn't name for fear they'd sneak under all his bands of control, for fear they would *win* and ruin everything.

Matilda opened her eyes, fixed him with that beautiful violet gaze, her mouth curved. "How long have you thought of me this way, Javier?"

"I wish I had never thought of you this way," he replied quite honestly. Because she should never have any doubts where they stood. He didn't want to actively hurt her. Maybe his honesty would, but it was better than lies and deceit. He had been up-front from the beginning and would continue to be.

"That doesn't answer my question," she returned. "I was thinking…sometimes, in the old days, you'd touch my hand and I'd feel this…*thing*. It felt dangerous, so I shied away."

"You should have continued to do so."

She sighed, not in exasperation exactly, because she

smiled when she did it. But the feeling was close. "So you say. But I quite enjoyed myself, Javier. And you seemed to as well."

Enjoyed was not the word. It was far too simple. Far too tame. And he could not answer her question, because he did not know and did not wish to.

Sometimes, those times he'd seen her during the three years she'd dated Pietro, he had felt an odd prickle at the base of his skull. A frustration with Pietro's hand in hers. A searing pain at the way she looked up at the other man so adoringly.

It was that which had led Javier to look deeper into Pietro in the first place. To find out all the lies the man had told her, fooled her with. To find out his true intentions.

He'd tricked himself into thinking it was just the due diligence that Ewan would have requested of him. But now, in this moment, he knew.

He just hadn't wanted the marriage to happen. And he'd never know, if Pietro had been completely innocent, if Javier wouldn't have concocted his own reason to stop the wedding.

A terrible, concerning thought.

"Are you going to stand there scowling at me all night?" she asked, smiling indulgently. Like she could read every last thought in his head. Like she knew this weakness inside him.

But one thing she clearly did not know was the darkness. She did not understand that she'd opened herself up to it. That he had to stop all this lest the cycle continue.

He opened his mouth to tell her that she should get

dressed and return to her own quarters. To *dismiss* her. Certainly, he had no intent to slide onto the bed himself.

So he had no idea how it turned out that this is what he did. Gathered her against him and tasted her once more. Kissed her until she was writhing against him, until he was hard again, until she murmured his name, wanton and pleading.

But it was she who broke the kiss, who pushed him back though not away. Her gaze traveled down his body, and she wriggled her way down his chest, planting kisses and featherlight touches that had whatever he'd been about to say or do or feel evaporate.

"Cariño mío—"

But she waved him off. "I want to know everything."

It was a strange way of putting it. He didn't like to think of her with Pietro, but they'd been together nearly three years. Surely she'd done "everything" with that slimy bastard. Though she likely hadn't had any male companions during her stint in Scotland.

But he forgot all about Pietro, and everything, when she touched him. Her hand, followed by her silky mouth. Greed over seduction, curiosity over experience.

It did not matter. The sight was too much. She was too much. He was hurtling into a hell that felt too much like heaven. He knew it was a lie, a trick, his own personal downfall, and yet he didn't stop her.

He watched her. Encouraged her. Those violet eyes meeting his. Her mouth full with him. It would haunt him all his days. The pleasure. The pain. He tangled his hands in all that wild flame of her hair, guiding her.

Never again would come tomorrow, and tomorrow would be here soon enough.

Mattie woke up Javier's bed, warm and cozy and a little sore in places she had never once been sore in before. But even in that ache, there was a delicious satisfaction.

She inhaled deeply and let it out slowly. She knew she would not roll over and find him smiling, happy, interested in seeing where all this heat could go. There would be no cheerful or excited plans for where a future could lead.

He'd said *never*, and she did not doubt him for a moment. She was not a fool. Or maybe she was, because she wanted to understand *why*, and had no doubt any attempt would be thorny and painful.

A smart woman let this be this—a wonderful experience to keep her warm and satisfied all her days—and walk away. Maybe she should settle for Vance. Maybe now that she knew all two bodies had to offer each other, she could… replicate it in some way with another man.

But even having never had another experience like this, there was no way to have it with anyone else. Javier meant something to her. It was complicated, and not something she'd fully worked out yet, but it was there.

She turned to him. He lay very still, but his eyes were open. His expression was harsh, closed off, and he held his whole body tense. But he did not say a word, did not attempt to send her on her way.

He just *lay* there.

She studied the scars that marred his muscled frame. Some were jagged, some were small, but they were all there on his torso. She thought of what Elena had told her, and how obvious these scars existed only where they could be hidden away.

She wondered if Javier would tell her…or if he would lie.

She reached out, brushed her fingers across the longest one. "Where are these scars from?"

If possible, he tensed even more. "Where do you think, Matilda?"

"Your father?"

"Indeed."

He didn't need to say much more for her to finally understand in full why her father had meant so much to Javier. Why he felt such a debt to the man. It wasn't just that Ewan had been kind to him, that her father had supported him in university and business.

It was that Ewan had offered him and his mother peace and safety where they hadn't had any before.

Mattie couldn't even begin to imagine the complexity of feeling that must come from that situation, and she doubted very much she would ever get Javier to speak of it. If she did, it would certainly not be *now* with her naked in his bed.

So she changed the subject, tucking this one away to a time he might be more receptive. "Everyone who knows me calls me Mattie. Except you."

"And so it shall be always."

"Why?"

He rolled off the bed on a sigh. He did not look at her when he said the rest. "Because we are not friends, Matilda. And we will no longer be lovers after you leave this room."

She knew he felt that way. Considered agreeing. It would be the easiest course of action. But much like running away, she wasn't doing that any longer. Easy wasn't always *good*.

Sometimes the good things were very, very complicated and hard.

"What if I endeavored to change your mind on that score?" She flung the blanket off of her. Naked and spread out on his bed.

Heat leaped into his dark gaze, nostrils flared, and he curled those large hands into fists. Who knew she would have this kind of effect on a man like Javier? This kind of *power*. It was a heady thing.

Perhaps he didn't want to want her. Perhaps he fought all those impulses when it came to her because of her father or whatever other reasons he might have, but he *had* those wants and impulses. There was something about her that tested this man's impressive resolve.

"You will lose," he insisted. But he didn't prove that statement. He grabbed a shirt and began to pull it on. To get dressed and no doubt storm out.

All these times she'd thought him angry at her for something. Thought him turning away from her was designed to hurt, but she saw it for its truth now. Him walking away was never about her.

"I always thought you were so strong. So brave. Not afraid of anything. Certainly not the kind of coward who is always running away," she said, still quite comfortably naked on his bed. Maybe she should find some embarrassment or shame or timidity, but with Javier…with everything he'd done to her over the course of the evening, she couldn't muster anything other than a smug kind of confidence.

And a new understanding of the man she'd for so long misunderstood.

He stopped abruptly in his retreat, his spine stiffening

as he turned to face her. His expression was fierce, and still every inch of him tense and ready for some kind of attack. As if he couldn't quite believe this was just…nice.

"Cowardice." Then he laughed, low and bitter, making her…well, have a *few* doubts about what she'd said, what she felt.

"*Cariño*, I could spend the next few days using you up. Discard you once I've have had enough. It is a kindness that I walk away from you. Time and time again. Perhaps, for once in your life, you should have the good sense to accept my kindness."

She wouldn't let his harsh words get to her. She would focus on the fact he had considered "using her up" at all. "I quite enjoyed the kindness you showed me last night."

"They always do." His smile was mean then.

But it was a mask. It was meant to hurt her, or at least throw her off. But she could hardly be jealous because she'd had no claim on him before.

Well, if she thought too much about it, perhaps she felt a twinge of jealousy, but not in the way he seemed to think she would. Not in a way that would hurt. It wasn't a bitter envy. It was more a wistfulness that they could not have found each other sooner.

But they could not have. She understood this fully, regardless of what happened from here on out. She had needed these past few years. She had needed her heart broken and to realize just what she did when she failed. She needed to understand her own cowardice, and now that she did… It just didn't seem all that hard to be brave.

It was quite possible he needed more time, and she considered she might even be able to give it to him. But she wouldn't be a coward while she did.

She went ahead and climbed off the bed herself. But she did not worry about her clothes—they were in the bathroom anyway. She simply tugged one of the soft blankets off his bed until she could wrap it around her body.

If he wanted to engage in games, two could play. "I suppose I will see if Vance has messaged me then." She made to set out into the hallway and down to her quarters, though admittedly she prayed she wouldn't run into any staff naked under but a blanket, but if she could make a dramatic exit, she'd risk it.

He grabbed her by the arm instead, stopping her forward movement. "You will not play games with me, little girl." His eyes flashed.

But she understood the anger that radiated off him was not at her, or even her attempt to make him jealous. It was all about whatever was going on inside him. And that...that she couldn't heal for him. He would have to figure some of it out himself.

"It's not a game, Javier," she said, very calmly. "I am endeavoring to give you what you want. I offered myself, you have refused." She lifted her shoulders, attempting to keep her voice calm and vaguely patronizing. "I will not beg."

"You did last night."

She smiled at him. "So did you."

His scowl deepened as he dropped her arm.

Which brought her *immense* satisfaction. This entire strange turn of events did. Perhaps because as left field as it might have seemed if someone had told her this would happen even a few days ago, it felt perfectly right.

Like they'd always been walking toward this moment—whether either of them liked it. Well, Matilda liked it. She liked *him*, for all his faults. But at the core of all those faults was something good. That good thing had just gotten… warped somewhere along the way.

A need to protect. Her. Himself. A need to control likely born out of a childhood where he must have had very little. Because no doubt if Javier's father had *scarred* him, the man had also hurt Elena. And Javier would have borne witness to that.

Poor little boy. Poor Elena.

How long had he held on to those scars, those fears, those traumas? Held tight and polished into something he could bear.

She had never felt particularly protective toward Javier. Never understood that underneath all that…self-assured armor was someone who clearly just needed someone to… care. To *take* care.

She knew he wouldn't welcome that from her, but that didn't mean she couldn't offer it all the same. And solve some of their problems while she did.

"Here is what I think, Javier. We know and like each other, most of the time. Clearly, we have chemistry. I don't know why I'd bother throwing myself at a parade of men when *we* could be married and likely be quite happy at it."

"Happy? You still believe in fairy tales after everything that happened to you, Matilda?"

"I don't believe happiness is a fairy tale, Javier. I think I've learned that it's a choice. And I think it's one you're afraid to make."

"You would speak to me of fear again?"

"Yes," she replied simply.

"You are terribly misguided, Matilda. And hear me now. I will never marry you. No matter what circumstances arise. I will never, *ever* marry. Not you. Not anyone."

So vehement. So sure. Clearly a decision he'd made long ago. But she could not fully fathom why marriage was such a non-starter to him. Particularly if he considered it a fairy tale when it could also be a friendship, a business arrangement, a facade.

She tightened the blanket around her but didn't cower. She smiled up at him with all the compassion whirling around inside her and asked the simplest of questions she knew he would not want to answer. "Why?"

CHAPTER FOURTEEN

JAVIER DID NOT know why the question struck some deep chord within him. A vibrating, painful ache. When the answer was simple, and something he'd always known.

She shouldn't question it. She was delusional. Whatever experience she'd had with Pietro must have been subpar at best and she was rendered a little senseless by what an exceptional lover could do.

That was all.

So there was no need to go into the reasons he would not marry her. He was Javier Alatorre. He no longer explained himself to anyone. He simply *acted*. He demanded. He *commanded*.

But no matter how certain he was he should not answer her question, he still stood here. Looking down at her. The push and pull of an internal argument inside him.

He should not tell her. He should shut her out.

But if she understood, perhaps she would stop pushing. Perhaps she would stop…

She would never stop. He could not afford delusions about her now. Now that he had done that which he'd sworn never to do. Now that he had to…regain control of the situation.

Because perhaps he had faltered, but he would not fail. He would not simply tear into pieces because he'd taken one misstep. Allowed one misguided *want* to derail that which needed to be done.

Matilda. Married to anyone but him.

So he would make it clear. This wasn't about all that *fear* she kept accusing him of having. It was about all the things someone like her could never understand. Should never understand.

"You know what I come from now, Matilda. I shouldn't have to explain why marriage is impossible."

She got that look in her eye, all determination mixed with something he didn't know how to label. There was a softness to her determination, a vulnerability. The fact that she did not yet know how to hide those was infuriating.

She should be stronger. More in control of herself. She should wield better armor so he could not pierce it any more than he already had.

"But it is not impossible. You've just decided you don't want to do it. And if it's not solely about me being Ewan's daughter—which would still not make it impossible. Actually, the opposite, if I really think about it. But if it's about *ever* marrying *anyone*, I am going to need an explanation."

"I owe you nothing."

"Does everything have to be a debt?"

She was talking in circles. In riddles. Like she was running about digging up all the foundations that kept him upright, so that he was crumbling.

But Javier Alatorre wouldn't crumble. Never again.

"My father was a monster, as my mother told you. He

caused the scars on my body, because he was physically abusive toward the both of us."

That softness in her settled in her violet eyes as they deepened with care, concern.

He wanted none of these things from her. They made him feel weak. Small. Like the little boy who'd cowered in a corner hoping never to be found. Hoping to avoid the blows. Sometimes even wishing it would be his mother in his stead—the monster was her choice, after all, was he not?

And those thoughts, those memories, made him certain of his choices. It made him certain of everything.

It wasn't just the man he was biologically connected to who was a monster.

It was Javier as well.

"It is very clear. Scientifically. Statistically. Children of abuse are more than likely to repeat the cycle. To be a danger to anyone and everyone they come into contact with. I could be selfish. I could gather up anyone and everyone I wanted. I could procreate however I pleased. God knows, plenty do."

Matilda nodded, as if she understood. As if she could. And it made him angry. It made him shake, deep within, with all that violence he'd been handed down. Perhaps he had learned how to control it, but he would never take the chance he might take it out on someone.

Particularly Matilda.

"But I looked at the studies, I looked within myself. I decided to break such a cycle. To let it die with me. So there will be no marriage. There will be nothing. The monster dies here."

Matilda did not nod. She did not cry. She did not agree. She looked confused. "But you are not abusive, Javier."

"Just because I have not used my fists on you, *cariño*, does not mean you know what I am or am not." Who could know?

"You are *not* abusive," she insisted. Missing the point entirely. As he'd known she would. This was why he should not have tried to explain it to her. Explanations never led anywhere safe, controlled. They never led to anyone understanding that which he *knew*.

So he said nothing. After a while she sighed and shook her head, but she did not leave. She stood here in his space, in what was his, and infused it with her scent, with her soft voice, with too many memories of last night and what she felt like under his hands, under his mouth, clouding his mind.

"You speak of studies. Data. But did you ever speak with someone?"

"I interviewed—"

"No, Javier. Did you speak with anyone about what happened to you? Your mother? A friend? A therapist? Have you dealt with your own experience in any way? Or did you simply find the potential effects and decide to control the universe, so they did not happen to you?"

He pictured icy waters. He envisioned the entire room encased in it. To fight the tide of hot, dangerous anger. She needed to leave. Even in his anger, his fury, this uncontrollable thing that felt too close to panic, he would never *show* her what he was.

That was the gift of control Ewan had given him. "I have done that which I thought best," he said coolly, envisioning himself in a boardroom. Giving a speech to his team. Not her. Not in his room, his sheet.

"That is not healing, Javier."

Healing? Why would he want that? "And you would know? With your silver platter and perfect father?"

"He wasn't perfect. Nor was being a motherless child. No, I cannot imagine it left the same scars as what you went through, particularly with the cushion of wealth, but let us not pretend my life has been so perfect I could not possibly understand pain that needs healing."

"It is of no matter, Matilda. I have made my decisions. I will not change my mind. I apologize if last night gave you a false sense of—"

She barked out a laugh, standing there wrapped in his blanket—which should be so utterly ridiculous not alluring in the least. "Oh, Javier. Do not pretend. To apologize. To know what I feel. You do not even know yourself."

"And you do?"

"Not completely, no." She moved forward then, and he held himself still. An iceberg himself. Nothing and no one inside. Just cold. Just ice. Even when she put her soft, warm hand on his chest. "But I would marry you, and I would take care of you. And I would never, ever fear you." She inhaled deeply, watching him with those soft violet eyes. Her exhale danced across his face.

She might as well have stabbed him clean through with the sharpest blade she could wield.

"I do not think you are a monster. For all the ways I have been angry at you, frustrated with you, confused by you, I have never been scared of who you are as a man. I know you would not hurt me in any of the ways you fear, and

I know that… It must be very hard to believe that about yourself. I wish I could do it for you. But accepting that you are a good man worthy of anything is going to have to be something you do on your own."

"I will not."

She nodded, a little sadly, but certainly not as she had years ago when she'd found out about Pietro. Hollow-eyed and lost, like a bombing victim. *That* had torn her to pieces, and that tearing had been what had allowed herself to hide away in Scotland for so long.

He'd always told himself that. He'd given her time because of the great hurt she'd endured. He'd never allowed himself to consider he'd allowed it because her far away from him was easiest. That distance put to bed any temptation.

He shook that thought away. It didn't matter if it were true, if what he'd told himself was at odds with his true motivations. All that mattered was that Pietro's betrayal had destroyed her.

His refusal of her suggestion they marry didn't even put a dent in her. Didn't that prove everything he needed to know right there?

"For as long as I'm here, my bedroom door is always open to you, Javier. And the potential that we marry and attempt to make something of whatever exists between us as well." And with that, she left his bedchamber, his own bedsheet trailing behind her.

Opening too many doors that should remain shut. That *would* remain shut. He would bolt them himself.

But her words stuck with him for too long. Like a thorn in his side, this possibility that wasn't a possibility. *I would never, ever fear you.* An impossible little flight of fancy. Perhaps she would always have it, but he would not.

But perhaps she was right about one thing.

He controlled the universe.

So he arranged for Vance Connor to come to dinner here. He would push her toward him. The man she *could* marry.

And would have to.

Mattie returned to her room. She felt a mix of so many things it was a bit exhausting. There was a certain amount of selfish joy that she'd finally shared her body with a man, and it had been beautiful. Wonderful.

Pain enveloped her when she thought of all the good things that Javier could not see in himself. Frustration that he'd block any chance of happiness away because of *statistics.* Because instead of getting help, he'd determined locking his true self away was the only safe option. His fear—

No, she realized. Like everything else, this was simply an excuse. He wasn't afraid of being a monster. He thought it was true. Whether he'd ever lifted a hand toward anyone or not, he saw the man in the mirror as a monster. As the father who'd abused him.

Mattie did not know what to do with that. She was no therapist, no mental health professional. How did you reach beyond someone's trauma to their heart, and all they could be if they believed it?

She had no clue. More, as many doors as she'd opened with Javier last night, she also understood that this was…a tangle. They'd started with sex instead of understanding. Maybe even beyond that, Javier couldn't meet her with understanding until he extended some to himself.

She considered calling Elena but did not know how to talk to the woman about having sex with her son, or about this without admitting to that. It was too delicate and tricky.

But that left her no one to really talk to and that struck her as sad. Pathetic, really. But she only had herself to blame, because she'd cut everyone else off these past three years.

She let that sobering thought depress her through the duration of her shower, but by the time she got out and got dressed for the day, she'd made some different choices.

The past three years had been anchored by wallowing, disassociating with plants, and isolating herself from every hard discussion, decision or feeling she possibly could. She would not repeat those steps here. She had to find different ways to cope.

So instead of gardening today, she called one of her old friends from school and set up a lunch get-together for later in the week. She left Javier's home—only informing Luis of her plans because she could not find the driver and did not have her own car here. She went into Barcelona and let herself wander, participate in life around her. Enjoy. She went to the botanical gardens and spent an hour befriending a volunteer there—an elderly man who listened to tales of her garden with great interest and showed her things he thought she'd like.

She did. All of it. She went to lunch by herself, chatting with the quirky waitress at a charming little bistro. She stopped by Mrs. Fernandez's house with a bouquet of flowers and was invited in for lemonade and conversation about her many grandchildren.

She wished there was someone she could speak to about

what was going on with Javier, but this was the next best thing. *Life*. Not isolation. Not fear. Just life.

As her father would have wanted for her.

This thought led her to take a little stroll in the Parc de la Ciutadella, as she'd once done with her father in the summers. And she didn't feel angry for his ridiculous will stipulations. She just missed him, and felt him there, walking with her, as silly as that was.

When Matilda returned to Javier's home, she felt like a new person. Maybe it wouldn't last, all these epiphanies, all this optimism, but she was going to follow it for now, and try to carve out this new idea of how she wanted the next few years to look.

Not isolated *in* Scotland, though not isolated from it either. Balance. Somewhere, she had to find some balance.

And so did Javier. She couldn't do that *for* him, but maybe she could find some way to nudge him in the right direction.

She barely opened the door to her rooms when Carmen pounced.

"We must get you ready," Carmen said, disapproval of what Mattie had chosen to wear on her afternoon out written all over her face.

"For what?" she asked as Carmen tugged the bags from her hands and set them down on the ground.

"For dinner."

"I have no plans for dinner."

"Mr. Alatorre is having guests over, and your presence is required."

"Required." Mattie sucked in a breath. What would *this* be about? Something designed to irritate her, no doubt. She considered being petulant and refusing, but Carmen already had clothes—ones Mattie had not brought from Scotland or anywhere—laid out on the bed.

"You may choose yourself," Carmen said as though she were making some great peace offering when the choices were both nearly identical. A simple black dress with sleeves, or a dark navy dress that was sleeveless.

Mattie would have preferred some color, so she grabbed the navy and disappeared into the bathroom to change into it. It fit perfectly, of course, even though it wasn't from *her* wardrobe, and she had no idea who'd procured it or when.

She let Carmen choose her jewelry and fuss with her hair. Mattie did some minimal makeup herself, much to Carmen's chagrin.

"With eyes like that, you should use what makeup offers as a weapon."

"With eyes like mine, I don't need weapons," Mattie replied cheerfully. She didn't let herself think about what guests Javier might have invited. She refused to let the little wriggle of anxiety win.

Carmen studied her. "You seem different, Miss Willoughby."

"Mattie, as I've repeatedly told you. And I feel different, Carmen. I feel really different." Different enough to march downstairs full of confidence and bravado and only a little tickle of uncertainty. She followed voices into one of the sitting rooms.

She stopped short, recognizing the man standing next to Javier at once. "Vance."

Vance turned to face her and smiled. Standing here in Javier's home, in Javier's orbit. She didn't know why it struck her as so wrong, only that after the events of last night she didn't know quite how to behave around him.

Which was ridiculous. They'd shared a few dances and some conversation over the course of one evening. She certainly shouldn't feel any guilt for what had happened with Javier last night, or any discomfort that they were now all in the same room.

He crossed and took her hand. "It's good to see you, Mattie."

Mattie. Because he'd listened to her request and filed it away. Unlike Javier, who wanted to keep her at a distance.

Maybe this was the kind of thing she needed to be paying attention to. Maybe this was all the sign she needed. Vance was willing to put forth an effort. Javier was not.

Vance brushed a kiss over her knuckles. It should have been nice. It should have been welcome. But her gaze moved over to Javier.

He inclined his head. As if to say *your move*.

And she knew there would be nothing *nice* about this evening Javier had set up. Particularly when a stunning woman—the same woman from the charity gala—entered the room apologizing for being late and brushing a kiss across Javier's cheek.

A clear sign, or perhaps *shots fired*.

But Mattie had no need for a battle. She understood his need for one stemmed from fear, and she wasn't afraid of him.

But he was afraid of her, and that was something to hold on to.

CHAPTER FIFTEEN

JAVIER HAD TO grit his teeth to keep from snapping at Ines. She kept yammering on and on about the artwork on the wall of the dining room and Javier was far more interested in hearing what Mattie and Vance were chatting so intently about down at the other end of the table.

As they should be. As was his intent. And regardless of anything that had happened last night—because it would be best if they both forgot the happenings altogether—she seemed to enjoy Vance's company.

He tried to focus on Ines through dessert, but knew he failed. He could feel her displeasure radiating from her and yet his gaze could not seem to be ripped from the couple at the other end of the table.

It felt so much like those years Matilda had been with Pietro, those times he'd been forced to share their orbit at society functions…until he'd finally figured out how to know if she and Pietro planned to attend.

He didn't like the clarity now. That all those years he'd convinced himself it was just some…protector instinct, developed only for Ewan's sake, in Ewan's memory. But it was jealousy. Plain and simple.

As though a few years had matured him enough to

see past all his own excuses. No matter how he tried, he couldn't convince himself this roiling frustration inside him was distrust or distaste of Vance. He couldn't seem to believe these feelings were about protecting her.

It was about *wanting* her. Damn his soul to hell.

So he was taking care of it. Vance here for dinner, ensuring they made more plans to be together. He would ensure they spent all the time together needed.

But next time he wouldn't be here to witness it. His hand clenched into a fist under the table as Vance leaned over and whispered something in Matilda's ear that made her laugh. Those violet eyes sparkling for another man.

He wanted to bash the man's perfect teeth in. He could picture it. *Feel* the slap of bone against bone. His heart raged for that physical fight he had no right wanting.

Because he was a monster. Violence was his blood. Who else would imagine fighting a man for simply talking to the woman he could not seem to excise from his being? Who else would have to hold himself back from storming across the room and taking that which he wanted?

Her. Her. Her. Last night in his bed. In his shower.

He was a tangle of too many sharp feelings, and this was the perfect example of why he would find a way to get her married off to Vance before the month was over.

For her own good. Her own safety.

"Javier?"

Javier blinked, looked over at Ines. Her mouth, usually curved in some kind of flirtatious expression, was a straight line. She touched a hand to her temple. "Unfortunately, I'm coming down with a bit of a headache. I should take my leave."

"Of course." He knew etiquette demanded he walk Ines outside and tuck her away in his car to have his driver take her back to her apartment in Barcelona proper. But he hesitated, because he hated the idea of leaving Vance and Matilda alone together, even though that's exactly what he should do.

Ines stood abruptly, the chair scraping back with enough force both Vance and Matilda looked up from their oh-so-intimate conversation. Ines threw her napkin on her plate and began to stalk out of the room.

"If you'll excuse me," Javier muttered at Matilda and Vance's surprised faces.

He followed Ines out of the room and told himself it was good to have an excuse to leave. To stop having to witness Matilda's red hair tilted toward Vance's perfectly straight white teeth.

But the minute he was out of the room, following Ines's retreating form, he wondered what they would do now that they were alone. Would Vance put his hands on her? Would she allow it?

It became harder to breathe. Impossible to focus on anything but the idea that Matilda might press that beautiful, lush mouth to anyone else's mouth. That she might let another man's hands touch her perfect, velvet skin.

Fury boiled inside him like the inherited disease it was. He could control anything, the whole world, but this was the ticking time bomb inside him. *She* was going to be the thing that finally detonated it and he could not allow it. Would not allow it.

Ines had stormed all the way to the front door, though she did not exit it right away. She turned to him then, not looking the least bit pained from a headache. Her expression was all anger. "What was tonight all about?" she demanded.

He blinked, trying to bring his thoughts away from Matilda and to the woman before him. "It was a casual dinner. As I said when I invited you."

"Are you really this...delusional? I don't need to be your wife, Javier, but I won't be your plaything when other women are involved."

"There are no other women involved," Javier replied darkly.

She laughed, but it was not her usual laugh. Carefree. Seductive. No. This was harsh. A sign he'd miscalculated greatly when he never did. Especially with women.

Still, she did move toward him in what he might have termed a seductive move. She put her hand to his chest, tilted her chin up to meet his gaze. "Then kiss me, Javier."

He looked down at her. Offering her mouth to him. It wouldn't be the first time he'd kissed Ines. The time they'd spent together had been enjoyable enough. He rather liked her when he wasn't...distracted.

"I thought you had a headache," he said instead, and knew it was perhaps the lamest response he could have managed.

Her hand dropped. Her expression turned to icy anger. "Have your driver meet me out front. And do *not* follow me outside." She wrenched the front door open, but offered one last parting shot before she closed the door behind her.

"You need to figure yourself out, Javier."

Then the door slammed shut, the sound echoing through the large entryway.

But there was nothing to figure out. Not for him. And

once he got Matilda out of his home, he could go back to his normal life. He would have control of everything that raged inside. The monster would be leashed once more.

He just had to get rid of Matilda. Once and for all.

Mattie walked through the gardens with Vance at her side and wished he was someone else. No matter how nice, how handsome, she could not seem to eradicate thoughts of Javier for him.

The entire meal she'd felt Javier's gaze on her. Not Ines. Not his meal. *Her.* And though she had tried very hard to focus on Vance, had sometimes even succeeded, far too often her thoughts had drifted to last night.

She talked about the gardens with Vance a little bit, about some of the art he was interested in. They had nice conversations.

Everything was *nice*, and a few years ago she might have leaned into that. Been happy and satisfied with that. Because there was nothing *nice* about what she felt for Javier.

But that sharp, edgy, dangerous thing Javier offered had altered her. She could no longer settle for nice. For safe. She needed to face the dragon, so to speak.

"Why do I get the feeling I'm in the middle of a game I don't know the rules to?" Vance said quietly.

"It's not a game." Mattie sighed, feeling a mix of guilt and frustration. "Not that I know *what* it is, but it's not meant to be a game. Vance…"

She stopped walking and so did he. She looked up at him. He was so nice. He was exactly the kind of man she *should* want. But all she could think of was Javier.

"I'm sure it's complicated," Vance offered, kindly. So kind.

She nodded.

"I prefer simplicity myself."

"I used to think that too."

"What changed?"

"I'm not sure exactly. Maybe I stopped hiding from myself. Maybe my life just can't be that simple." She wanted to give Javier a taste of that simplicity. She wanted to give him all the kindness he didn't think he deserved. She wanted… him. Plain and simple. So it wasn't fair to pretend otherwise with Vance. "I'm very sorry. This was never meant to be some kind of…leading you on."

"I think I understand that." He lifted her hand, much as he had when he'd greeted her. Brushed a kiss across her knuckles. "I'm sorry it couldn't work out, but I wish you the best of luck, Mattie."

"You too, Vance."

"I don't suppose you could introduce me to Javier's date?"

She laughed. "I'll see what I can do, but I have faith that you can secure your own dates."

He shrugged, his expression amused. A nice man, and she couldn't even pretend to want him. What was wrong with her?

"I'll walk you out," she offered.

Vance shook his head. "No need. Goodbye, Mattie."

"Goodbye."

She let him leave on his own, because there was just not enough pretending in the world. She wanted Javier. Both physically and as a man. She wanted to…help him. He clearly had things he needed to work out that he was refusing to, and she wanted to somehow lead him to a place where he dealt with his trauma so he could… So he could understand he was not doomed to follow his father's footsteps.

What a sad fate he'd given himself.

She found a bench, much like the one she planned to put in her section of the garden eventually, and settled herself onto it so she could enjoy the smell of flowers, the nighttime whisper of plant life. She considered if this was some misguided need to change him or was it a more honest wanting to help because she cared about him.

Had she simply latched onto Javier now because he was in a strange way safe?

She laughed to herself in the darkened garden. No, nothing about Javier felt safe. He made her forget herself. He made her want things she didn't fully understand. He frustrated her beyond reason and made her say and do things that felt like someone else.

These were not bad things. In fact, for *her*, in this moment, they were good things. Not that long ago she'd viewed a loss of safety like a loss of life. But that was a sad, isolated way to live. To never risk. To never try for something that scared her.

She was done withdrawing or isolating from that which felt too scary. She was realizing there was no reward without risk.

Would she have ever realized that if Javier hadn't made her come here? If Elena hadn't pointed out her withdrawal tendencies?

She wanted to believe that she would have, but maybe sometimes people came into your life to teach you something, and maybe she could teach Javier something in the same vein. All his control, all his personal belief he was a monster, was only his own version of withdrawal.

He needed to be brave. She nearly laughed again. He got so offended when she accused him of cowardice, but he was *made* of it.

"What are you doing out here?"

Mattie had to squint at the dark to make out his outline. Standing there. As if he was afraid to get close. "Thinking," she offered.

"Why did Vance leave?"

Mattie let out a long sigh. "He is not a stupid man, Javier. Any more than Ines was a stupid woman."

"What does that mean?"

She got up off the bench and walked over to him. He stayed in the shadows so she couldn't quite make out his expression, but she could all but *feel* the war inside him. Stay or retreat.

Either would make her happy. Because both responses were about how he felt about her. He wanted her, no matter how little he wanted to.

"They both knew that all we could think about was each other. No matter how hard we tried to do otherwise."

"Do not fool yourself into thinking you know what was going on in my head."

She laughed. Probably too loud as that man she'd already forgotten the name of had accused her of doing.

"Oh, so you weren't thinking about the shower last night? My mouth on you in your bed? You weren't chastising yourself for wanting Ewan's daughter? For this foolish notion that you're some kind of monster like your biological father?"

"I was dreaming of beating your date to a bloody pulp," he said, so darkly. Clearly so certain that would shock her.

But it didn't. Because he seemed to not understand a very basic tenet of life she'd learned when she'd been a little girl. Struggling with how she felt about the fact she couldn't remember her mother, or that her father wanted her to go to boarding school, or those first few difficult months testing out Elena as a stepmother and what that meant. Or even these past few days, being so angry at her father for leaving her this ridiculous will stipulation.

"But you didn't even lift one finger to him, Javier. You did not hurt him, threaten him. What does it matter that you thought of it? Thoughts aren't actions."

He shook his head, there in the dark, so she kept moving toward him. Until she was close enough to touch. She wanted his hands on her, his mouth on her. She wanted the wild ride of last night again because she'd never felt quite so free, quite so herself, as she did when he touched her and made her forget everything.

Safety. Danger. Grief. Fear. Worry.

It was all burned to ash when he was inside her.

She reached out, put her hand to his chest, and said things she never would have dreamed she'd have the courage to say to anyone. "I want you. I can't stop thinking about wanting you. Your hands on my body. The way you taste. The way you make me feel."

"I told you what I am, Matilda," he growled. And she understood that growl was him attempting to control himself.

But it was a *fight*.

She realized he thought it all the same. *Any* impulse was wrong, would lead him down the path of his father. So he fought them all, used his control as armor. It was why he wanted no one in his space. Why he kept himself in his own controlled little worlds. Why even his gardens had to be neat, tight rows. To hide this monster he thought he was.

But that was not him, or he would not have hugged her in his office the other day. He would not have taken care of her finances, devoted himself to her father's wishes, kept everything she'd run away from going while she'd been off in Scotland.

No, he was no monster, but she did not know how to prove that to him. Except this. And maybe that was selfish.

But she didn't care.

"You think you're a monster, but I don't. I guess you'll have to show me."

He reached out, tangled his hand in her hair, then fisted it. "Do you think I won't?"

His grasp on her hair was tight, and perhaps she was some kind of monster too, because it sent a thrill through her. Deep and throbbing. "I hope you will."

CHAPTER SIXTEEN

SHE WAS POISON. She was life. She was his downfall and when his mouth was on hers, he could not find himself. There was only want. There was only her.

She pressed against him, and he held his hand curled in her silky hair so that he could move her mouth at whatever angle he pleased. So he could move her head out of the way, so he could set his mouth to her neck, use his teeth.

And it didn't seem to matter that he let go of every scrap of restraint. That he was rough with her, desperate and lacking all control. She did not stop him, did not push away, did not tell him no.

She egged him on. She kissed him back with teeth, held on to him with nails. And then…she begged him. Explicitly and desperately so that he didn't even concern himself with the fact that they were outside.

He pushed up the skirt of her dress, pulled down the underwear she wore. He settled himself on the bench, moving her with him and then settling him on her lap. He thrust inside her, no finesse, no seduction. There was no time. Only the roaring of everything cascading inside him. War. Battles.

And she accepted him so easily, so perfectly. He'd barely

moved at all when she came apart like she was as desperate, as lost, as big a fool as he.

He pulled at the bodice of her dress until he freed her breasts, naked to the air and him. Dimly he heard the fabric tear, but it did not penetrate, because she was begging. Making little noises that snapped any last hold on control he had. He feasted on her while she writhed against him, rode him. Hard and wild. Her skin glimmered in moonlight like water. Her pleasure played out over her face, the river of her hair like magic all around them.

She shattered again, and still, he didn't stop. She slumped against him, his name on her lips, but he simply shifted her, until she was splayed out on the bench.

She was flushed, her eyes seeming to glow here in these shadows. Watching him. He should go. Escape now. With what little glimmer of sanity he had left.

But she trailed her own hand down the length of her body, arched her back and made a long, contented sound. Her eyes never leaving his. "More," she whispered.

More, more, more.

It echoed in his head, a need he could not resist. He gripped her hips, settled himself inside her.

"Do not hold back this time," she said. "Give me everything, Javier. *Cariño mio.* Everything."

So that everything he'd ever known, ever held on to, ever believed evaporated, and there was only the tight, perfect glide of her body against his. The ecstasy of letting loose and letting go, pounding every last ounce of emotion into her until she was screaming out his name, and he lost himself in the sound of it. In her. Emptying himself until there was nothing left.

He *shook*, there on top of her. Outside, where the air seemed to slowly cool around them as his breath, as his mind, as his *sanity* returned. He withdrew from her, his head ringing.

She had ruined everything. Fully now. There was no recovering from this.

"Well," she said, somewhat cheerfully, as if anything about this moment could be *cheering*. She sat up, tried to smooth her dress back into place, but the bodice was ripped. Her hair was a riot, impossible to tame. No one would see her and not know exactly what had happened to her.

A flame within tried to fan to life again, but he quashed it. He'd ripped her dress, been rough with her. Perhaps it had not been unwelcomed, but she did not understand. She… She…

She confused everything. Crumbled walls he'd crafted over *years*. He could not let her get beyond those walls and dig up his foundations too.

He stood, tucking himself away. Trying to find something to hold on to. Some grip on control.

She ruined everything, so she couldn't be here anymore.

"You must leave, Matilda." How could she not see that? How could she think this could continue and not be the ruin of everything?

"Where would I go? Back to Scotland?"

"You should go find Vance. Apologize. He seems a good man. I have not been able to find anything wrong with him. You should do what you can to make that work."

"But I only want you."

He had never felt quite so cleaved in two, quite so many emotions batter him. It was pain and it was…longing.

No matter how little he should, he only wanted her too. But it could not be. It would not be.

"You are mistaken," he said, trying to find the icy control he'd once known.

She laughed. "I know you are the only man I've been with, and I know I'm supposed to think that's childish, but it isn't. It's just the way things—"

But none of the words after *only* seemed to penetrate. A low, dim buzz began in his ears. "What did you say?" he rasped. "I am not the only man. I... You and Pietro were together for years."

Her brow furrowed. "We were, but we never shared more than a kiss. He did not...want me in that way. He dressed it up in many different things, waiting for marriage and whatnot, so we never... Javier, you are it for me."

He felt like a soldier on a battlefield struck by a bullet. Like he might simply keel over, dead, at any moment.

This could not be. Too many things tried to crowd in on him. Her initial discomfort in the shower, the inexpert way she had touched him at times. But he had ignored all those things because she had not given them any credence. Because...because... He had known it couldn't be. He had just assumed Pietro had been useless in *all* things.

It couldn't be. But she'd said it so offhand. It made...too much sense. And made so many things immensely worse.

He had broken a sacred trust already, but he had not known...that he would have...debased her in such a way when she was innocent. She'd come to him untouched, and he'd marked her, stained her, ruined her.

Monster.

"If you will not leave, I will."

"Javier…"

But he did not hear anything else she said. Could not. He was striding for the house. Was he running? Everything inside him was galloping. Wrong.

This was so wrong, and he needed to escape.

Mattie sat on the bench in the garden for so long she was shivering by the time it occurred to her to stand up. She did not understand what had just happened, and she certainly did not know how to fix it.

He'd run away. Actually *run*. It wasn't even cowardice this time. It was fear, straight through. Like she was some kind of threat. To his very life. From the look on his face, she might have thought she'd stabbed him clean through. But all she'd done was told him what she'd assumed he'd already known.

Honestly, she could not fathom why that made anything different. Whether she'd ever had sex with Pietro or anyone else or not, what changed?

"Men," she muttered. Honestly, that was the only explanation for that one.

She walked back into the house, quietly slipping back into her quarters. She wasn't quite certain how she felt. The moment had been glorious. The aftermath had been…confusing. All that being glad she'd pushed him to the edge now felt…sadder, somehow.

He'd run away. Like a boy. She did not wish to hurt him—not with what they'd done, or what she'd said, but how could she have predicted it would have such an effect?

When she got to her room, she didn't bother to change

out of her ripped dress. She just sat on the bed and tried to work through…anything she was feeling.

Part of her wanted to run back to Scotland. Hide in her plants. Withdraw from all this complication. It was a tempting safety.

But she had changed. Because even as she felt that wistfulness for isolation and safety, she knew she could not choose it. It would not solve any of their problems. And Javier was a problem she did not want to ignore.

She wanted to fix whatever issue was between them. If only she fully understood the issue.

It was such a strange feeling, to be so new at bravery and not hiding away, and now see someone do…exactly what she'd once considered a mature, healthy move. Javier wouldn't likely hide the way she had, but he would run. And run and run, until he came up against something that made him realize the truth of what he was doing.

She couldn't help but have some concerns he never would. Her experiences had been so tame if she compared them to his. Didn't that mean he'd need a much bigger and scarier wall to run into him for him to realize anything?

He'd told her to go. Should she? She wouldn't go cuddle up to Vance. It wasn't honest or fair to a nice enough man. But she *could* give Javier the space he so desired. Leave him to figure it all out on his own.

That is what he'd given her years ago, and even now, knowing it hadn't been the healthiest choice, she was grateful to him for it. Just as she was strangely grateful for him seeking her out, being so bound and determined to see her father's wishes seen to.

Sometimes, time did heal, or help the healing process

along. Sometimes, time was needed to fully change, mature, to be ready for the changes and maturity that waited.

But she didn't want to give Javier time. *That* was selfish, she knew. What she didn't know was what the right choice to make was.

But maybe there was someone who did. She called Elena. And she told her…not everything, but enough. Not that she'd engaged in a physical relationship with Javier, but that romantic feelings had been introduced. Not that Javier thought himself a monster, but that he had misgivings because of…so many things.

"He told me I had to leave, and I… I don't want to, but shouldn't it be about what he wants? I don't want him to be unhappy. I don't want to the source of…this pain."

"You aren't the source, *mi niña*. You are the wall you speak of. He has hit it, and now he must make a choice. Change, as he should. Grow, as he should. Or close down even harder. So, you must stay put," Elena instructed. "He will expect obedience, and you must not give it to him."

"So what *do* I give him?"

"Do you love him, Mattie?"

The question was asked gently, but Matilda felt as though the gentleness was for Javier, not herself. She had been very careful not to use the word *love* with Elena, with Javier, even in her own thoughts.

But it had hovered there. Just another fear she wanted to ignore. Because love still scared her. She had thought she'd loved Pietro, but it felt nothing like this. She had thought love was safe, easy. Not scary, not painful.

"I know you were happy with my father. I know he loved

you very much. Javier does not think you loved my father," Mattie answered instead. "Is that true?"

"Of course not," Elena replied. "Javier saw… He saw the misgivings I had about *myself* as misgivings I had about loving your father. He cannot separate the two, and he would not let me explain it to him when I finally understood it."

He cannot separate the two.

Mattie thought on that. On what she'd seen out of her father and Elena. It did not *look* painful and conflicted, but she had been too young and kept out of it to know how they'd been together in the beginning.

"Your father was very patient with me, because he loved me even when I did not love myself. Oh, Mattie, I hope you'll be patient with Javier if you love him. He needs it."

Mattie realized Elena was giving her an out, not forcing her to answer the question she'd avoided. Maybe she should have told Javier first, but part of her felt as if she owed the truth to Elena here and now, because she was his mother, worried about him.

"I do love him, Elena," she said, though her voice shook. Not with doubts. With worries that she wasn't strong enough to be as good and patient as her father had been. But she would try.

Because for all Javier's faults, she loved the man he was. His strength, his dedication. The way it felt as though they were equals, as though they could help each other be better versions of themselves.

She could be his safe place to land if he let her. He'd already been hers. Even when she hadn't fully realized it.

"Then that is what you give. You cannot control him.

You cannot change him. These are changes he will have to decide on his own. But if you're there, if you refuse to let him convince you otherwise, then maybe he can find the safe space to finally...face himself."

"And...what if he doesn't?"

"You decide how deep that love goes, Mattie. You cannot decide anything *for* him. Only for you."

Mattie thought of those words all night, and then all through the next day when she couldn't find Javier. And when finally one of his staff members told her he'd gone and would not be back for some time, she realized she had a lot of choices to make.

For herself. Once and for all.

CHAPTER SEVENTEEN

JAVIER HAD LEFT. Not just his estate, but Barcelona. He could not bear…any of this. Whether Matilda listened to him and left as well, whether she was stubborn and stayed, he could no longer be in this place that he'd cultivated as a sanctuary.

She'd ruined it.

He wasted no time packing, telling Luis to book a flight. First, he flew to London, convinced he would do some business at the WB offices there. He spent the entire morning making mistake after mistake.

It was of no use. He could not seem to find his control, his focus. Everything was scattered in a million pieces.

She'd ruined him.

He left the offices before the day was out. He briefly considered another WB office but knew there was no point trying to work. He could go to his holiday home in Capri, but what would he do there? Fume. Pace. *Think*.

No, it would do no good. So he flew back to Spain. But not Barcelona.

Valencia. Where his mother lived. He did not know what possessed him, felt even more confused when the driver pulled up to her smaller more traditional beach house, surrounded by luxurious modernity.

She could have had a bigger house, a staff. Though much of Ewan's wealth had gone to his daughter, the man had made sure both Javier and his mother would always be taken care of no matter what. Javier had built on what he'd been gifted, creating his own dynasty.

His mother had seemed to be content with what was. Demanding something small, artistic and cozy right on the water, until Javier had given up trying to talk her into something better.

He paid the driver and got out. The night air was warm, and he could hear the water crashing against the beach, though the dark and houses blocked any view of the gulf from here.

He stood in the front yard, staring at the way it *did* exude coziness, here in the dark. A few lights on in the shadows, wind chimes tinkling in the breeze. He had avoided this as much as he could. Often going to great lengths to convince his mother to come to Barcelona if she wished to see him.

Why? He asked himself now when he'd never questioned himself before. Why had he insisted she come to his estate, and why did he suddenly understand every complaint she'd leveled against it? Too big. Too cold. A *mausoleum*.

This too was Matilda's fault. These realizations he didn't want. Making everything he knew to be right feel wrong. Breathing life into the gardens of his estate if nothing else. Understanding the beauty there and refusing to see the lack of life.

Because she was the life it sorely lacked.

Javier marched up to the door and knocked. He would demand Elena handle this. Talk to Matilda. Get through to her. Stop…whatever it is she was doing to him. He could not, clearly, but Elena could.

His mother answered the door. Her mouth went slack with surprise. "Javier." She looked behind him as if expecting someone else to be with him. Her gaze returned to him on her porch. "What are you doing here?"

And all his demands, all his certainty, just seemed to evaporate. He felt lost. A child again. When they'd finally escaped that monster and there had finally been peace and he hadn't known what to *do* with it.

So he'd gone to the streets and found war. Until Ewan. Until a man had looked at him and seen potential instead of a curse.

"I did not know where to go," he managed to say. Because it was true. He had no idea where to go, to be. No idea how to solve this horrible pain within him.

She made a tsking noise, then pulled him inside. All the way to her cozy kitchen, which was much nicer than anything they'd had in the slums of Madrid, and yet it reminded him of being a teenager all the same. Coming home after a fight, bloody and bruised and surly.

She spoke to him in Spanish as she had then, words of encouragement and endearments as she fussed in the kitchen, preparing tea, even though he had not told her the problem. Back then she would have patched him up, begged him to find some good instead of some bad.

He realized back then she had been desperate, afraid. And that was gone. She was calm and collected as she made tea, as she assured him all would be well even without knowing what was wrong.

He had convinced himself he'd come here to have his

mother set Matilda straight, but the minute he'd seen her, that had changed. And now, in her quiet and supportive chattering, he realized what he really wanted. Needed.

Matilda had opened up some small kernel of hope inside him, so he'd gone to the one person who knew enough to help him quash it. His mother might have infinite hope in him achieving bigger and better, but she knew him. She knew what it was.

The hope had to be extinguished. That was the only possibility any of them survived.

"Do you remember my thirteenth birthday?" he asked, interrupting whatever she'd been saying about better days ahead.

Elena paused in her movements, before straightening her shoulders and turning to face him. He could tell that she did. That it lived in her head as it did in his.

"I need you to explain that to Matilda. She will not listen to me."

But his mother's expression turned to one of confusion. "Explain what?"

"What I am."

"Javier, *mijo*, I don't follow." She crossed to the table, a mug in each hand. She put one in front of him, then sat across from him with her own. Javier knew from the smell alone it was Ewan's favorite blend.

That old familiar pang of loss rippled through him. Too much to bear under all the rest of this upheaval.

So he had to quash it. By remembering the day he least wanted to. By reminding himself, his mother, *everyone* who he was underneath all the control he'd built inside himself.

"My thirteenth birthday. When you tripped, and you

dropped the cake you had made me. Even though he'd told you not to. I was so angry that I couldn't have even that. So I… I was going to hit you."

"You did not hit me," his mother said with vehemence. The same kind of vehemence she'd once used to insist his father had not been wrong.

Because they were the same. She would defend him as she'd once defended his father. "I raised my hand to you. You knew what I intended. You saw what I was capable of."

"Is that what you think?"

"It is what I know." He had seen the horror in her eyes. He had seen everything in her change. He had seen himself then. Fully clearly for the first time.

As bad as the man he'd come from. Evil. Bleak. Lost.

"I was not scared of you, Javier," his mother said so sincerely.

But she was wrong. Misremembering, lying. *Something.*

"I did not think you would actually hit me. I lived with an abuser…my whole life. My father hit me. Your father hit me. It was all I knew. It is why I stayed so much longer than I should have. I thought it normal. I thought…he was right, *they* were right. This was how someone learned."

She had never told him that before. That her own father had also hit her. But this just proved his point. Abuse was a cycle. She had been born into it, chosen it. Then she'd left— escaped. Because the only way to break it was to remove yourself from it. She'd removed him from one part, and he would remove himself from perpetuating it in the future.

He just needed someone to explain that to Mattie.

His mother leaned forward, placed her hand over his fisted one on the table. "When you were very young, your father only hit me. But as you got older, he became more focused on you. It was all I'd known, so I did not stop him, but it…it felt wrong. I did not trust my own feelings then, so I simply lived with that wrong. I did not know better, and still, I carry that heavy burden of guilt everywhere I go. I do not know that I will ever forgive myself for this, but through therapy I have learned to give myself some grace." She managed a shaky smile. "Ewan was part of that grace."

He made a move to get up, to remove her hand from his. To escape this talk of…*grace*. But Elena's grip tightened.

"That day, when you lifted your hand to me. So angry, so upset. Because yes, you couldn't even have this small thing. You were a young man who had so little. But that was the moment my eyes were opened, Javier. Not to…whatever it is you think. That you are some kind of monster? No." She said this with a kind of disgust that pinned him to his spot. Almost as though…she'd never thought that of him.

When how could that be?

"It is when I saw you…so conflicted. So horrified by your own actions that you *did not want* and did *not* act on. It was an impulse you controlled, at thirteen. Something your father, a grown adult, had never done. My father, also a grown man, had never stopped himself from doing. You did not swing that hand. You did not yell at me. You lifted that hand in a spark of fury, and then you dropped it the next instance as if your entire world had ended. Right there."

Javier tried to find the words to tell her she was wrong. She misunderstood. He'd wanted to hit her because his blood was tainted. Because he was in an inescapable cycle unless he kept everyone at fist's distance.

But he remembered that moment too well. The riot of

feelings inside him. Disgust. Horror. He had not wanted to hit her. It had been a spurt of anger and the only way he knew how to deal with anger at that time was violence.

But no part of him *wanted* it.

What did wants matter? If he was capable of lifting a hand to his mother, even if he'd resisted the impulse, he had all the potentials of a monster inside him. Of this, he was sure. Until his mother kept speaking.

"I knew I had to get you out. I had to leave. I did not understand then what physical abuse could do to a boy. What it had done to me. I thought it was all normal. But I understood in that moment the emotional abuse we were putting you through, and I spent the next six months planning our escape so that it would not continue. We owe everything that came after to that moment. So I remember it. Clearly. As the turning point that saved us. *You* saved us, Javier."

"You planned the escape." He had never given his mother enough credit for that. Partly because he had not understood the depths of…trauma she must have faced, the way her world had been warped before she had a chance.

And if he gave his mother grace… He shook his head. This was too much. She was…muddling everything in his head. He wasn't here about the past. Even if it informed his future. It didn't have to be about the cycle he would no doubt perpetuate. His mother just didn't understand.

"Javier. What is this all about? Just what isn't Matilda listening to you about? That you're some kind of villain? You have been a fine guardian to her. I know she wasn't pleased about leaving Scotland, but it ended up being good for her." His mother paused, her hand still on his. "Javier, I think *you've* been quite good for her."

That was the breaking point. He pulled his hand away from his mother's grasp. Stood. Paced. It was clear Matilda had told his mother *something*. And neither of them understood. But there was something they both needed to.

"Ewan would have never wanted me for her. It is a disgrace to his memory. It is a *disgrace*."

"Did it ever occur to you that this is exactly what Ewan wanted? For the both of you."

Javier stared at his mother for a good full minute, possibly without drawing a breath. "No," he finally managed. "No, of course not. That is…that is insane."

"Is it?" Elena asked, sipping her tea. "The stipulation is not that Mattie should marry *anyone else* by the time she was twenty-five. The stipulation was that if she did not, you would have to marry her."

"Yes, but…"

"There are no buts. He put that in there because he always thought about what a fine full-circle thing that would be if you two found each other when you were both old enough. I know he'd hoped to have been here, hoped that the will would never have been used in such a fashion. But don't for a second believe that if he *was* here, he wouldn't be finding clever little ways to put you in each other's orbit. He never would have forced your hands, pursued it, if it was clear as adults you didn't suit, but do not for a second think he wouldn't have wanted it. I *know* he did."

"That cannot be true. He… He must not have known about… He could not have known that I…"

"He knew everything about you, Javier. And he loved you all the same. You know this or you would not be so dedicated to his memory. His wishes. But if you are dedicated to the ones you understand, you must also be dedicated to the ones you don't. You are the only one who fancies yourself a monster. You are the only one who is worried you are not good enough."

"I am *not*."

His mother studied him for the longest time. In silence. For a few moments, he thought she finally understood. That she would finally agree. That he could be free from this vise in his chest. This pressure and pain and loss of control.

"Do you know why it took so long for me to agree to marry Ewan?"

Javier did not understand this change of conversation. "You were friends. You needed money. A better future for me. You… It was a marriage of friendship, of convenience."

She laughed. Threw her head back and *laughed*. "*Mijo*, truly, you have been so dedicated to these fictions you've created. I loved that man. Deeply. And he loved me. But I was afraid, and I was traumatized, and it took time to work through that. I wish I hadn't let my fear of facing it win for so long. We could have had more years together, but I cannot go back and change it."

Javier shook his head. No. It was not love. They'd had an affection for each other. They had been *friends*. For years his mother had resisted Ewan because…because…

Afraid and traumatized.

He didn't know why he was so committed to not believing they loved each other. Only that it made everything inside him more complicated, more confusing.

But he could see the way Ewan had been around his mother. They were not overly affectionate in public, no. But there'd been an expression Ewan's face had gotten when his mother entered a room.

It reminded him of Matilda. The way she'd looked at him under that arbor, or in his office that had once been Ewan's when she spoke of the locket he'd given her for her sixteenth birthday.

Elena took his hands, like she was imploring him. "Don't make my mistakes. Do not resist love because you think you're not good enough. Do not resist trying to find healing because of the amount of hurt it takes to get to the other side. Don't waste time, Javier. I wasted so much time. But those years I had with him, really had with him, were worth everything. If you have feelings for Mattie, you must deal with them. And it has little to do with me, your past or Ewan. It has nothing to do with being 'good enough'—whatever that means—it has everything to do with your heart."

"I do not have a heart."

"I once thought that about myself. That it had been beaten to pieces. Burned to ash. I failed you for thirteen years. How could I deserve love? I was wrong, Javier, and so are you."

He wished he could argue with her, but that heart he did not want ached in his chest. A foreign thing, soft and vulnerable. He wanted to shore it up with all the armor he'd learned how to build since he was a child.

But he couldn't muster it. Not with his own mother's regrets laid out between them.

And still there was so much fear. Matilda was…light and…

"What if I…? What if I hurt her?"

"You will. In ways you can't predict. And it will hurt. No

amount of control can take away the fact that we're human. Hurting each other doesn't make us monsters, it makes us fallible. What matters is that we apologize, that we seek to make amends. I have never not seen you do this, Javier. You can be a hard man, but you are not a cruel one. No matter what you've convinced yourself of."

"You do not know…"

"You are my son. I know."

He wasn't sure he'd ever heard his mother speak with such certainty. Except maybe her wedding vows to Ewan. A man she'd loved. Not just used as a means to escape poverty and struggle.

Javier did not know what to do with any of this. He wasn't even sure of who he was anymore.

But he supposed… He got to choose. He was in control. And if that was the case, maybe he would choose…

Not to be a monster.

If Ewan, if his mother, if Matilda could not see the monster within him, then maybe…maybe it was not something to be quite so scared of.

CHAPTER EIGHTEEN

MATTIE HAD STAYED put in Javier's house. She had spent the days of his absence deciding what she wanted her life to look like. As much as she loved her cottage and gardens and experiments in Scotland, it wasn't a *life*. A vacation, maybe. But she needed...more.

She went to a volunteer training for the Coalition of Rural Safety. It would require some travel, some fundraising, but it would give her something to do and feel quite useful doing.

Beyond that, she'd thrown herself into her garden. She'd ordered a trellis and bench, discussed obtaining some new plants with Andrés. She would leave her mark on these gardens if nothing else.

Every time she thought of leaving, finding her own space here in Barcelona, she came back to what Elena had said.

You decide how deep that love goes, Mattie. You cannot decide anything for him. Only for you.

The choice to leave was not for herself. It was for him.

When she thought of leaving, she realized the aim was to make him more comfortable, to punish him, but never because leaving was what *she* wanted.

So she stayed. She was elbow-deep in soil, plants, her

newly constructed trellis and contentment three days after he'd disappeared when she heard foreboding footsteps approach. She didn't turn right away. She didn't want to get her hopes up, and she wanted to have some control over herself if it *was* the man she wanted to see.

When she felt steady enough, she looked over her shoulder. "Ah, so you're back."

He said nothing, just stood there all brooding and beautiful. She looked back at the dirt on her hands, then decided to finish what she was doing. He would have to determine the course of the conversation if he was just going to walk up and tower over her like this.

For a few minutes, all was quiet. She could tell he hadn't left, but he said nothing, and she continued her work, humming quietly to herself.

"Is this the clematis you were wanting to plant?" he asked by way of greeting.

She stopped what she was doing, looked up at him again. Was that some kind of…peace offering, remembering the plant name she'd brought up that evening they'd eaten dinner out here?

He took a deep breath, slowly let it out. His gaze was fierce, his hands curled into fists, but there was something in him that made her hold herself very still. For good or for ill she did not know.

"We need to talk, Mat… Mattie."

A jolt went through her. Surprise and a spurt of joy she immediately tried to tamp down. Just because he'd used her nickname didn't mean…anything.

But of course, it did.

She sucked in an unsteady breath. He had said, very emphatically and not that long ago, he never would.

Carefully, she tugged the gardening gloves off her hands, then got to her feet. She turned to face him, trying to find some look of impassive disinterest—until he explained what this was. "About what?"

"I have been visiting with my mother."

She frowned a little, confused by this admission. "In Valencia?"

He nodded.

"But you almost never go there."

"I did not originally plan to. I went to London. I tried to work. And then I went to my mother so that she would tell me, tell *you* in a way that would get through to the both of us that I am no good for you."

Mattie snorted in derision. "What a fool's errand, Javier."

"Yes, it was. She did…quite the opposite, I suppose."

Mattie blinked. What was the opposite of that? *Being* good enough for her? Wanting to be?

Javier stepped forward, closing the distance between them. His dark eyes glittered with something she could not quite read, but he took her hands with a gentleness they had not often shown each other.

"I cannot control myself when it comes to you. I wanted it to be only physical, but I have never felt this way before. I have never been haunted, poisoned, *obsessed*."

"These are not nice words, Javier."

He made a sound, almost a chuckle. And it warmed her, even if those words hadn't. Because he did not chuckle easily. He did not do any of this…easily.

"I have controlled everything in my adult life, except

the loss of your father, and except for how I feel about you. Years ago, when you came and told me you had said yes to Pietro, I suddenly realized… I wanted it to be me."

He said this like the confession had been beaten out of him. Like it was potentially one of the worst things he'd ever done. When it settled in her like warmth. Like joy. Back then, when she'd been so young and foolish, he'd wanted it to be him.

"I did not know how to… It felt wrong. When you were my ward. When Ewan had entrusted your future and safety to me. I had no right to you, even if I was a good man, and I very much did not feel as though I was."

She freed one of her hands so she could cup her palm to his face. "I have never thought you a monster, Javier. I cannot imagine I ever will. Maybe not perfect, but who is?"

His gaze met hers, dark and fierce as always, but with a searching intent she'd never seen there before. "I cannot bear the thought of you marrying anyone else. Now or six months from now."

She beamed up at him. "Then I guess you'll have to."

"We could forgo the stipulations. If you wished. You were right, back in Scotland, there is no real legal ramification if you refuse. I will not hold you to this. I want you to be happy."

For a moment, she worried he didn't want to marry her. That she was misunderstanding. But that was fear. He was here. He was saying these things. "I don't wish. I would be happy to marry you."

His mouth curved. "Just like that? You would marry me? No reservations. No concerns."

"I have known you my whole adult life, Javier. I spent

years being afraid of or uncertain of what feelings you brought out in me. But I don't hide anymore. I don't run away. I know the man you are, and I know the woman I am. We will have our issues, no doubt, but I have faith that we can sort them out."

He dropped her hands, framed her face with them instead. His gaze tracked over her features, something like awe in his expression that made her feel…perfect. Like every moment had led her here. Where she belonged.

"You know, my mother even suggested that…that your father might have wished it this way."

Everything inside of her went cold. Her *father*. She thought it was about her, about them and… And it wasn't at all. She thought her chest might cave in.

She pulled out of Javier's grasp. This wasn't real. It was all about her *father*? What a fool she was. What a fool she *always* was.

"What is the matter?" he asked gently.

She took a step back. The words were too hard to find, and if she ran…she could just turn and run. Go back to Scotland, not face this. This horrible, horrible hurt. She would refuse him and never have to marry anyone and—

But she was not that woman anymore, so she fought the urge. She lifted her chin, met his gaze. "Now that you think it has my father's blessing, it's just okay? You don't have to love me, care about *me*? As long as you're fulfilling *his* wishes? Well, no, Javier. I won't marry you to make my father happy."

She blinked furiously at the tears welling up as she whirled away from him and started to storm away. Inside. She would pack everything up right this minute and—

"I would marry you to make the *both* of us happy. Me. You."

She stopped abruptly. Had she heard those words correctly? Her heart was galloping, and there were tears in her eyes and she felt…so many different things.

"I love you, Mattie. I have loved you for a very long time. I have endeavored to control you, control the environment when I was around you, and it worked when you were afraid of me—"

She turned to face him then, and a few tears spilled over. "I was never afraid of *you*, Javier."

"Very well. Afraid in general. What I feel for you, what I want our lives to look like, has nothing to do with your father. But knowing he might have approved…knowing he *would* have approved means something to me. I cannot deny that. Your father was…something of a true north for me. In a childhood of pain and suffering and what felt like wrong choices from everyone, he always seemed to make the right ones. I know he was not a perfect man, but he endeavored to be a good one, so I endeavored to…to mimic it. I am naturally not a good man."

"Stop that."

"I do not *feel* as though I am a good man, but I would like to…to work toward feeling that I might deserve you. Work toward deserving each other. And your father's blessing, according to my mother, is part of that. I'm sorry if that hurts you."

He used those words so infrequently. *I'm sorry.* Sounding so sincere, like he truly was.

She took a breath, trying to separate her fears from his words. Her *fear* was that he could only want her because of her father, but she knew better. Everything about the past few weeks should have taught her better.

She managed to shake her head. "No, it doesn't. I... worry that you could not love me for me, Javier. That is *my* fear."

He nodded. Did not invalidate her fear. Just nodded. "I will endeavor to show you every day. I do not want you to go, Mattie. I want you to stay. To marry me. To love me, and if you need time—"

Time? When she knew time was so fleeting. She cut him off by all but throwing herself at him and pressing her mouth to his. When she said those words for the very first time, she said them against his mouth, her arms wrapped tightly around his neck.

"I love you, Javier."

He held her there against him, tight and perfect.

"I want to stay. I want to marry you. Tomorrow, if you'd like."

His laugh rumbled through her like joy. Like a peace they both had found together. "I think my mother will want to be here, but we will do it. Soon." He pulled back a little. "I am still...working on all this. A work in progress."

She gestured at the spot in his gardens she had made hers. "Good thing I love those."

Then he swept her up in his arms and took her to his room—*their* room. In *their* house. And loved her into *their* future.

EPILOGUE

IT TURNED OUT to be a rather good thing they both agreed on a quick marriage, because Mattie soon realized that they had not taken any of the necessary precautions those first few times they'd come together, so tied up in their own issues. The push and pull of what they allowed themselves to want.

They were still learning things about each other. Still working through things. She and Elena had finally convinced Javier to see Elena's therapist in Valencia. The wedding was set for next month, and all was well.

But Mattie did not know how Javier would feel about a child *now*. Even as she felt ecstatic for a future as a family. Nerves. Joy. Hope. She could have kept it to herself for a while longer, seen a doctor to be sure before telling him.

But Matilda Willoughby, soon to be Mattie Alatorre, was no coward.

She found him in his study, frowning at his computer. "One moment, *cariño*," he murmured when he glanced up at her entrance.

She tried to wait. She really did. But she was nervous, and didn't know the right words, so she simply blurted it all out. "Javier. Those first few times we were together. We did not use any protection."

"I assumed…" He stopped what he was doing, looked up at her. "What are you saying?"

"A little bit earlier than planned, I suppose, but… We discussed having a family." Sort of. She had been quite clear that was a goal of hers, and he had not argued, though he'd said very little. He was still working through it and now they were just…

"Are you… Mattie." He skirted the desk and crossed to her. He took her hands in his, as gently as he had that day a few weeks ago when he'd finally told her he loved her. "Mattie," he repeated.

"I will need to go to a doctor, but one of those at-home tests confirms what I've been wondering."

He didn't say anything. She wasn't even sure he breathed. He didn't look devastated, but they had been working on him sorting through his feelings, verbalizing them and not beating himself up for the negative ones.

"You don't have to be happy right away," she said emphatically. "You can be conflicted. We have time."

He shook his head, but she wasn't sure what he was refuting. "Matilda, you must promise not to let me…" His voice was rough, and he couldn't get the words out, but she understood him now. More and more every day. The worry he carried, about cycles. About what he might be capable of.

But he was working on it, and she had no doubt he would be an excellent father. She had no concern for him hurting anyone he loved. Not in the ways he worried he would.

"Every promise I have is yours, Javier. I know you will worry, and I will likely find things to worry about as well, but you will make an excellent father. We will do our best as parents."

"I had a good example."

Mattie nodded, trying not to feel sad that her father was not here to see them be parents. Together. Javier pulled her close, kissing her cheek and stroking her hair.

"I have loved you too long, *cariño mio*," he murmured. "And even in that I could not have dreamed you would be the answer to everything. That you would open my future to everything." He laid his hand over her still very flat stomach, wonder and joy in his expression even with all that worry. Because joy was not the absence of concern, bravery not the absence of fear.

They had learned that together.

"Love is never too long, Javier." Love was everywhere and everything. The tie that bound them. The thread that tied them together and into a future.

Where they filled their estate with a family, full of love and laughter and tears and always the promise that, no matter what, they would love.

* * * * *

If you got lost in the passion of
A Diamond for His Defiant Cinderella
*then don't miss these other dazzling
Lorraine Hall stories!*

Hired for His Royal Revenge
Pregnant at the Palace Altar
A Son Hidden from the Sicilian
The Forbidden Princess He Craves
Playing the Sicilian's Game of Revenge

Available now!